THE POWER OF A LOVE SONG

THE POWER OF A LOVE SONG

T. WENDY WILLIAMS

Gallien G5 Publishing

Cover Design: Candice Kilgore
Author photo: Kim Taylor

First Printing, 2025

For Aunt Jan,
whose piano told stories
that words could not

Other Works by the Author

vii

Mile High Confessions
Happily Never After
Lost in the Music (book one of series)
A Melody for Madeline (book two of series)

One

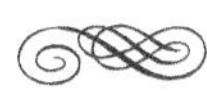

In Los Angeles, bricks hurled in frustration smashed through storefront windows. Homes and businesses blaze with flames out of control. Los Angeles Police Department choppers hover overhead, their rotor blades whirl, fanning smoke, dust, and debris. While nearly three thousand miles away in New York City, thunderous applause fills the air inside a dimly lit Paul Recital Hall. The spotlight, a celestial beam, shines on a twenty-two-year-old, Madeline May Richardson as she graces the stage. Although tears blur her vision, she sees her father, the Reverend Eugene Richardson, and his wife, Gilda, who's her manager and for three years now, her stepmother, sitting front row. The seat next to Gilda is vacant, reserved for Madeline's mother-in-law, Judy, who was scheduled to fly out the previous evening along with Melody, Madeline's four-year-old daughter. But then a verdict of not guilty was read in the trial of four white Los Angeles police officers who were seen on a home video mercilessly beating a Black motorist named Rodney King durring a traffic stop. Shortly afterward, hundreds of protestors surrounded police headquaters in downtown Los Angeles. Across town, unrest grew violent when locals, gathered at the corner of Florence and Normandie in South Central L.A., began attacking motorists. Months of simmering frustrations came to a boil from San Fernando Valley to Long Beach, blocking major throughways. Smoke from the fires grew so dense, flights were canceled.

Four years at The Juilliard School, and it all comes down to a key recital, yet each second proves agonizing, excruciating—like Madeline spent an entire night banging her head in frustration against a brick wall. There was hardly any time spent rehearsing—her mind was on the safety of her daughter, that of her in-laws, and the rest of her extended family. She imagined them watching from their pool terraces, billows of smoke darkening the skies. From her own television set, she watched in horror, neighborhoods and businesses perishing in flames. Guilt consumes her, gripping her like the hold of a constrictor. Forget a recital. She needs to be on a flight. If she can't fly directly into LAX, the John Wayne airport, located fifty minutes south, is the next best option. From there, she can quickly access the 405 and head north to her daughter. The minute she sees her, she's going to hug her. She can already picture herself burying her nose in her daughter's thick mounds of curly hair and inhaling her precious baby lotion scent.

The applause falls when Madeline sits before a grand piano, a Steinway with polished ebony wood. Her posture is erect. Her hair is swept into an intricate chignon with curly tendrils accenting each side of her heart-shaped face. The design of her black beaded gown clings to her curves and flows into a cascade of silk at her feet. The auditorium is now silent, save for an occasional cough. With eyes closed, she positions her hands on the keys and plays German composer Johann Sebastian Bach's "Partita in C Minor, BWV 826."

It's three minutes into the piece before she remembers it's been six days, sixteen hours, eleven minutes, and four seconds since she felt her husband, JB's touch. They spoke briefly last night over the phone.

"We need to be on a flight to L.A.," was how she started the conversation.

"But they're all canceled," was his reply.

"Are you sure?"

"Too much smoke in the air—not happening."

"Then what are we supposed to do?" The stressed tone of Madeline's voice had JB pacing the room of his hotel suite.

Opening her amber-colored eyes, she glances at the keys, striking each note. A tear rests on the tip of her nose. She closes her eyes again, and her thoughts drift back to JB. It's the NBA playoffs. He's a star player with the New Jersey team at an away game in Cleveland. From the start, distance and separation have been culprits woven into the fabric of their union. A wedding ring reminds her that she's still his wife, though she can't recall the last time she prepared a meal for him or separated and washed his dirty laundry. Something's brewing. Madeline senses it, though it could be stress related. Though it could be something far more. She reins in her thoughts to focus on the music. Her hands are familiar enough with the keys that playing them is second nature—like breathing, like blinking the eyes—her fingers dance, their urgency palpable. The piano groans, its strings vibrating with fervor. Bach, the composer, had captured the tumult of life—the storms that rage within the human soul. Madeline's eyes close briefly, her body swaying. She is no longer a pianist but a vessel.

Her heart flutters, remembering how she and JB clung together like spoons with his chest pressed against her back, their bodies covered in the dew and dampness created by intense lovemaking. Her musically trained ears delighted in the rhythm of his beating heart. Lying in JB's arms gave her a sense of protection and fulfillment. At six-eight, his arms are long and powerful enough to lift her one hundred and sixty pound, five-foot-three-inch frame effortlessly like a barbell. She relishes holding and squeezing him, feeling his firm, chiseled abdominals in her palms. His lips and tongue—bold and tender are familiar with every curve, line, and arch on her body. Every second is treasured until it's time to be apart. Yet, JB assures her in his playful, charming way, "Don't you worry 'bout a thaaaaang," in the vein of an old Stevie Wonder tune, and it's enough to get her through.

"What do we do?" He repeated her question. "Kick ass at your recital. I'll do what I do on the hardwood, then I'll call you after the game."

They hung up, and Madeline felt somewhat at ease.

While performing, she thinks of her daughter, Melody, and milestones she's missed. Madeline wasn't present to catch Melody's fall when she took her first step. Her mother-in-law knows Melody's percentage on her growth chart better than she.

The news coverage showed parts of L.A. looking like a war zone. There could be an earthquake happening, she didn't care. She needed to get to Melody.

Also in the audience, her piano instructor, Ms. Ivanov, listens to chord progressions—

a staccato here, a legato there. She's seen Madeline perform Bach before, but something is off tonight. She seems troubled. Ms. Ivanov's ears dissect Madeline's technique. The piece changes and gives way to Hungarian composer Fran Liszt's "La Campanella." Ms. Ivanov notes the emotional expression in Madeline's delivery in her grade book. Despite her performance this evening, she's seen Madeline's rigorous determination to execute a piece the way the composer would have. From the beginning, Ms. Ivanov recognized characteristics in Madeline's style and approach, which resemble the methods of those who've trained with Russian instructors. Unlike her other students whom she had to strip and rebuild, she dealt with Madeline in a more holistic approach. She learned Madeline's earlier days of piano instruction started with her mother.

When cancer prevented her mother from teaching, her mother insisted Madeline learn from the instructor who taught her piano. Ms. Pavlov, her Russian-born instructor, who fled the Soviet Union in the 1940s, during Joseph Stalin's regime, was well into her seventies but still active with piano pedagogy in the Houston area.

Madeline segues into a modern classical piece with Russian American composer Sergei Rachmaninoff's "Prelude in C# Minor Op. 3, No. 2." Madeline remembers Rachmaninoff had big hands; he could span twelve piano keys from the tip of his little finger to the tip of his thumb. She captures the sound the way he would have, reaching and expanding beyond her normal range. Her mother would've been proud. The thought brings a fresh round of tears. Her father, Eugene, notices them from his vantage point. Earlier today, he and wife, Gilda, stopped by Madeline's apartment for afternoon tea. She rushed into his arms like a scared little girl needing the protection and solace only found in a doting father's embrace. He prayed, with the expectation his words, along with his soothing tone, would ease her anxieties. "Psalms ninety-four verse nineteen says when my anxious inner thoughts become overwhelming, your comfort encourages me. Maddie, in times like these, you can always turn to God, for peace and encouragement."

"Yes, I know," Madeline replied.

"There's another verse: John chapter fourteen verse twenty-seven says peace I leave with you; my peace I give you. I do not give to you as the world gives. Do not let your hearts be troubled and do not be afraid. Do you understand?" he asked.

"Yes, Daddy. I understand," yet her tone was flustered and doubtful.

Frustrated, Eugene wondered how he managed to reach thousands with his message of God's love and the wonderful works of Jesus, but his words failed to penetrate the heart of his only child.

Watching her perform reminds him of the choice he made as her father and a man of God. If only he had been more present, she wouldn't have gotten pregnant at seventeen. Before that summer in 1987, Madeline was immersed in piano and performing at concert halls all over the country. That summer, she decided she wanted to take off, relax and be idle. If he had not allowed her to go to L.A., how different her life would have been. He wishes Madeline's mother, Evelyn, was alive to see this performance. Holding his current wife's hand, he brings it to his lips for a kiss. Even Gilda's scent is reminiscent of Evelyn's. They were best friends and so much alike. Though she's been dead for nearly a decade, there are still times when he calls Gilda Evelyn's name.

When the last note plays, Madeline feels a sense of relief. The audience stands to its feet with applause. She rises and takes a bow. The energy she receives from the audience is enough for her to forget the riot happening in L.A., if only for the moment.

Minutes later, Ms. Ivanov approaches Madeline, who awaits backstage. Ms. Ivanov's sternness gives her a commanding presence. No words or expressions are exchanged. The rhythm in the clicking of their kitten heels is the only indication of the meeting that is to come.

"How do you think you performed?" Ms. Ivanov asks once they're inside a small meeting room and she closes the door.

Madeline feels her palms and other parts of her body perspire. Her heart races, acting as if it's about to leap out of her mouth. Mrs. Ivanov sits behind a desk and lays out a small binder containing her notes. In the seconds of waiting for Madeline to answer her question, Ms. Ivanov notices trails of dried tears on Madeline's face.

"Something troubling you?" she asks.

Madeline was never one to allow her personal life to interfere with her studies, no matter how difficult.

"I need to fly to L.A. It's a family emergency," she tells Ms. Ivanov.

"Emergency?" Ms. Ivanov's eyes narrow as she reads Madeline's body language.

Madeline hesitates. "Yes."

"If there is such an emergency, why are you here?"

"It was important that I do this. Right now." It's shortly afterward when Madeline realizes how foolish it must sound.

"More important than your family emergency?" Ms. Ivanov asks. The question rings like a resounding gong. It's one that begs a definitive answer.

"My family means the world..." Madeline feels fresh tears stinging her eyes. "This recital means a great deal to me, too."

Ms. Ivanov takes out a pair of readers and places them on the tip of her keen nose. It was always difficult for Madeline to guess Ms. Ivanov's exact age. She always kept her hair brushed in a powdery white bun. If she weren't wearing matte red lipstick, her lips would appear nonexistent, hence playing up to her lack of expression, her stern taskmaster reputation.

"I wished your pedaling was a little gentler and subtle, however, I have heard no other interpretation of Rachmaninoff's piece speak in colors and variations to the degree that yours have."

Madeline nods, but inside, the positive feedback on the Rachmaninoff piece is significant. She listens to Ms. Ivanov give further critique. Madeline's understanding of Ms. Ivanov is much clearer, unlike before, where she was listening more to how Ms. Ivanov was saying things as opposed to what she was saying due to her thick Russian accent.

"In Russia we say otlichno."

"Translation?" Madeline asks.

"*Excellent,*" Ms. Ivanov responds.

Madeline gives her a hug. Within seconds, all pent-up emotions release like a dam that's been collecting tears from the past four years.

"You've proven yourself," Ms. Ivanov says. "Now go."

Ms. Ivanov's approval is a nod from the universe itself. Madeline's smile lights up the area when she enters the reception. Her father, Gilda, and others from the school greet her with hugs and praises on the performance.

"You've made the grade. There's no doubt in my mind," Gilda says to her.

"I'm sure. But first things first, Gilda, can you please get me on the earliest flight to L.A. tomorrow?"

"Maddie..." Eugene takes her hand. "You've just completed a key recital, which means you are days away from being a graduate of *the* prestigious Juilliard. Enjoy this moment."

Madeline squeezes his hand and tries her best to enjoy every praise and compliment lavished upon her. All the faces in the room are nondescript—students, faculty, and locals from the city, some are Juilliard alum who've come to appreciate and share their thoughts on her performance.

Gilda notices the streaks of tears on Madeline's cheeks.

"Maddie, let's powder our noses," Gilda says. "We won't be long," she says to Eugene.

"Oh, I know the code word for meeting in the ladies' room." Eugene winks.

Once inside, Madeline looks at her reflection in the mirror. Staring back are almond-shaped eyes in need of rest.

Gilda checks out her own reflection as she runs a hand through her layered cut. Gilda's hair texture feels like cotton, with its golden-brown color highlights that complement her peanut butter truffle skin tone.

Madeline wets a couple of thick paper towelettes to dab at her face.

"I'll book you on the first flight out," Gilda says.

"Thank you." Madeline gives her a hug and a kiss on the cheek before resuming a further check of herself in the mirror. "I was thinking about Melody, JB, and of course, Mother."

"I was thinking of your mother, too," Gilda begins. "She used to tell me, 'My child has an anointing on her. One day she's going to bless the world with her gift.'"

"She said that?" Maddie stops dabbing and looks at Gilda's reflection.

"Yes."

The idea she needs to share her gift with the world is lodged in her consciousness. It keeps her pacing the floors of her apartment at three in the morning. For the past year, it has had her taking lunch meetings with a Pulitzer Prize, Grammy Award—winning trumpeter and agreeing to go on tour with him and his orchestra. But then there is Melody. She needs quality time with Melody...and JB—with his insatiable desires and impulses.

"I'm scared, Gilda." Maddie's words reverberate off the restroom tiles.

"And that's okay," Gilda says, coming forward to enfold Maddie in an embrace.

The restroom door opens, and laughter echoes. Maddie notices Gracie Turrentine. The light in the bathroom reflects the prominent deep, ebony waves of her hair. From the moment they entered Juilliard nearly four years ago, Madeline and Gracie were the toast of the conservatory. Gracie's instrument is her five-and-a-half octave vocal range. Madeline noticed she wasn't too shabby with the piano, either. Madeline also made a shocking discovery. She and Gracie were cousins.

As soon as she could, Madeline ran to her apartment to call her Aunt Mary, her deceased mother's sister, to share her discovery. There was a moment of silence. Madeline couldn't understand why Aunt Mary didn't share her enthusiasm about the news.

"We'll talk further about it when I see you," Aunt Mary told her. That wouldn't be the case because it was during a visit with Gracie to her childhood home in Bed-Stuy that she discovered the family connection. Philip Caleb "PC" May, who was Madeline's grandfather and Gracie's great-grandfather, was a successful businessman whose family was among the rarest of Black families in America with wealth dating back to the Reconstruction era. PC May had a wife and three children, the youngest of the three children is Gracie's grandmother. Just days after his divorce was finalized, he met and married Madeline's grandmother, Magdalene.

When Madeline accompanied Gracie to visit the family, they looked at pictures in a family photo album. Through sepia-toned photos, Madeline recognized her grandfather PC's smile. His stately appearance reminded her of Duke Ellington. He was close to eighty when she was born. There is a photo of her and Cassandra back home in Houston holding hands with their grandfather, his smile is wide and gracious. Madeline is on his right, not smiling but holding a melted ice cream cone, and Cassandra stands to his left, looking up at his face, also holding a melting cone. He died when they were ten and nine. Gracie said she never got the chance to know him, that he was mentioned sparingly. The day he married

Magdalene, it was as if his first wife and their children never existed.

Gracie hails from a musical family; her parents are accomplished jazz musicians. Her mother plays the piano. Her father is a guitarist.

"Gold-star performance. It felt like I was at Carnegie Hall," she says, hugging Madeline. "Hello Mrs. Richardson." She greets Gilda with a hug.

"It wasn't my best," Madeline tells her.

"Well, in the Bach piece, I noticed a slight variation in the Sinfonia. The tempo felt rushed," Gracie says. "I was sitting there thinking, something's off."

"I need to get to Los Angeles," Madeline tells her while trying to keep her composure.

Gracie's expression softens, and she nods in agreement. She's watched the news, "It's crazy what's happening there."

Madeline looks at her watch. It's minutes after the game tip-off in Cleveland. If she makes it across the Hudson River, home to New Jersey, she might catch the fourth quarter of JB's game on television. She says her goodbyes and sheds more tears when Eugene and Gilda get in the backseat of a waiting cab. She watches it pull away from the curb headed in the direction of their hotel near Central Park West. She walks across the street to a waiting 1992 Lincoln Town Car. The driver greets her before opening the door. Madeline sits inside and rests her head against a soft leather seat. The sedan heads westward on West 65th Street, driving past the apartment building where she spends her days when her schedule is hectic or she's too exhausted to take the ride to New Jersey. Neon lights off countless billboards and displays reflected in the town car's windows. The lush greenery of Central Park, the pedestrians, the hustle and bustle, the one-hundred-year-old bridges and tunnels soon give way to pristine vistas and million-dollar homes. She checks the numbers in her pager, recognizing the number belonging to the award-winning jazz trumpeter, Lynnwood Tremé. There's a European tour. His management team talked to Gilda, who along with Madeline's attorney looked over the terms of the contract. Madeline sees this as an opportunity to establish herself on the international stage.

The sedan coasts into a U-shaped cobblestone driveway. Exterior lighting illuminates a multi-level, luxury ranch-style home. The entrance is grand with a pair of Mahogany double doors adorned with wrought-iron accents. Above, a lantern chandelier casts a warm glow, welcoming even on the darkest nights. Inside, it's dark. The marble floor echoes with each step. She's alone. She drops her purse and immediately grabs a phone to call Judy in Los Angeles. The phone rings several times before someone finally picks up.

"Judy."

"Maddie."

"Where's Melody?"

"She's right here."

"I need to hear her voice."

She hears Judy tell her, "It's your mommy. She wants to speak with you."

Seconds later, "Hi."

Hearing Melody's voice brings more tears. It's the sweetest sound. The grandest of Beethoven's sonatas can't compare. Madeline cradles the phone in her hand, and gravity pulls her to the sofa.

"Mommy loves you."

"I love you," Melody responds then proceeds to sing a song she learned from a new children's show with a purple dinosaur "I love you. You love me."

Madeline closes her eyes and listens. When Melody ends one song, she sings another. She is her father's child, singing melodies. Madeline wishes time could stand still. It reminds her of moments spent with her own mother. The feeling of being surrounded by a love so strong and gentle, it's difficult to imagine being without it.

"That was beautiful, Melody." Madeline applauds. There is silence on the other end. She must've given the phone back to Judy.

"Today, Melody and I read a couple of books," Judy tells her.

"What is she reading?"

"The same books I used to read to her daddy, Dr. Seuss: Green Eggs and Ham, The Little Engine that Could, Where the Wild Things Are."

"Yes, I loved it when my mother read those stories to me, too. Thank you, Judy. I appreciate you and James helping us with Melody."

"James and I are doing what good Lolas and Lolos do."

The irony isn't lost on Madeline. It was her father who insisted she give birth. Meanwhile, JB's father, James, stressed abortion. "Where's James?" Madeline asks.

"He's around."

"Can you see what's happening right now with the rioting?"

"It's scary. It's the second day of rioting, and people are out of control."

"I need to see my child."

"The way things are, I don't know *when* you can."

"I'm not staying here, not when I need to get there." The line goes dead. "Hello? Hello? Judy? Judy?" She glances at the phone and checks the dial tone. She tries to dial the number and gets a busy signal. Her heart races. This isn't good.

Two

The season is over. The first time during his four years in the league, JB's team made the playoffs, only to be eliminated in the first round. He shakes hands, bantering with opposing players. Great sportsmanship reads well when millions are watching. However, losing sucks. Playing eighty-two games in the season and losing over half of them sucks. He gave his A-game throughout the season only for the team to fold where it really counts—downright discouraging. The losing streak seemed to originate during his junior year as a Trojan at the University of Southern California.

That cloud of misfortune carried over the following year, as a member of the United States Olympic basketball team, losing to the Soviets at the 1988 Summer Olympic games in Seoul, South Korea. Standing on that third-place podium watching the Soviets' red hammer and sickle flag hoisted to dominance was agonizing, and worst—flying home to the United States only to be welcomed with boos. To watch the press scrutinize every player on the team and see the look on his father's face. *Son, you can't win for losing.* JB's U.S. Olympic bronze medal is still in a box somewhere in the basement.

A sports reporter wants a post-game quote. A cameraman angles his camera in position. The reporter is a foot shorter than JB. He holds the microphone.

"JB, tough loss tonight. How are you feeling right now?"

The arena lights and the sweat from tonight's game have JB's tan complexion glistening and his high-top fade a dark, curly hive of ringlets. He takes a deep breath. "It's a bitter pill to swallow, no doubt. We fought hard all season, but sometimes the ball just doesn't bounce your way. Disappointing? Absolutely. But we'll regroup, learn from this, and come back stronger next season."

"You had an incredible season individually—career-high points, rebounds, and assists. How do you balance personal success with team goals?

"Individual accolades are nice, but they mean nothing without team success. I'd trade all those stats for a deep playoff run any day. My teammates—they're my brothers. We win together, we lose together."

"The fans are disappointed. What message do you have for them?"

JB looks directly at the camera. "To the fans who've been with us through thick and thin—thank you. Your support fuels us. We feel your passion, your heartbreak. Stick with us. We'll be back. And to the critics—keep doubting. We thrive on proving people wrong."

"What's next for JB? How do you bounce back from this?"

JB uses his towel to wipe away the sweat dripping from his face before answering. "I'll take some time to reflect, watch the tape, dissect my game, and find areas to improve. When the new season tips off, I'll step on that court with hunger."

With Cleveland's victory, the fans aren't rushing to clear out the arena. A boisterous crowd lingers near the team's entrance tunnel. An overzealous fan hangs off the side of the rails with his hands out, wanting to touch the superstar. The energy in the place is still on a high from the win.

"Maybe next season," someone screams over JB's shoulder.

"How about never," another person screams.

The jeering follows him into the tunnel, echoing in his ears.

Now the expression from years earlier of his father, James, is visibly etched in his mind. James missed the last two playoff games. JB figures he already resigned the outcomes to defeat. James was accustomed to winning and didn't let an opportunity pass without reminding JB of it. He was on the 1972 Los Angeles team alongside Wilt Chamberlain, Jerry West, and Elgin Baylor when they won the NBA championship. JB was there—a five-year-old taking in the frenzy, covered in purple and gold confetti.

JB looks around his circle. His best friend and fraternity brother, Caleb, who plays for a Detroit team, already owned an NBA championship ring, and he barely got playing minutes. Paul, another fraternity brother, who lives up to his nickname, Hollywood, is winning accolades at Cannes Film Festival and rubbing elbows with the likes of Steven Spielberg and Eddie Murphy. He even received an Oscar nomination for his first film out of the gate. JB will be a free agent soon. If New Jersey isn't fighting to keep him, he's taking his talents elsewhere, with a team whose players are as hungry as he is.

Win or lose, the press conference in the locker room is still a circus, with reporters asking the same questions a thousand different ways. Of course, a reporter asks him a question regarding free agency.

"It's a situation of let's wait and see what happens," he answers.

"If you get another offer to continue with New Jersey?" another reporter asks.

"Unless they present an offer I can't refuse, my options remain open," JB shoots back.

After the press conference, he chats more with reporters and signs a couple of autographs before he decides it's time to call

Madeline. He looks at the clock, and it's a quarter after ten. He finds a pay phone and makes a call to their home in New Jersey. The line is busy. He makes a call to the apartment in the city. It rings for nearly forty seconds. He calls home again. Busy signal. Next, he calls the separate line to the home office. Hopefully, she'll hear it and pick it up. He lets it ring well over a minute. He hangs up, second guessing whether he's dialing the correct numbers. He picks up and repeatedly dials all three numbers. Same result.

Why is she not answering? He sends her a page putting his jersey number in the code.

He shaves, showers, and gets dressed. He makes another phone call home with no answer. He grabs his team duffle bag, his portable CD player, and Locs eyewear and takes a quiet walk to the team's motor coach. Fans anxious for an opportunity hold out basketballs, Sharpie markers, paper, and promo posters. A female wearing a lacy white camisole underneath a black-and-white pin-striped jacket offers her chest. JB pretends he doesn't notice her; the Locs prevent him from making eye contact. He gets on the bus and banters with teammates. Some are already talking about their plans for the long summer. There are two spots left on the U.S. Olympic men's basketball team. His name is floating as a poten-tial candidate for a spot. With a dream team of players like Jordan, Johnson, and Bird, he's certain, if chosen, the team will win the gold. He opens his duffle to retrieve a leather-bound binder. Inside is a composition notebook. He's thinking he can write a couple of lines while the lights are on inside the team bus. Once the bus starts moving, lights out, heads nod. There might even be a snore on the thirty-minute ride to the airport. A picture of himself along with Madeline and their daughter, Melody, is tucked on the front page.

I put away the black book

Don't need it anymore
You made me fall hard
The minute you walked through the door

He was sitting in the front passenger seat of his best friend Caleb's car when he saw her stroll out of the airport terminal in a cool and confident way. The L.A. breeze tousled curly chestnut-colored locks across her rosy cheeks. When she tossed her hair back, he noticed full, glossy lips; an ample chest; and legs so sturdy that when she walked by, his mouth dropped open, and his eyes followed her every move. He immediately got out of the car to get a better look at her. He noticed her tiny waist, and his eyes traveled to her peach-shaped backside. When Caleb, her first cousin, lifted her up for a hug, JB's arms were open for her to greet him just the same. To him, she felt like one hundred percent Italian silk-imported Egyptian lace. He didn't recall her ever looking this exquisite before. He didn't ever recall looking at her at all. She was off-limits, his best friend's first cousin. Some boundaries you don't cross.

A day later, he saw her honey-colored butt cheeks peeking out from underneath the swimsuit she was wearing. He was checking out her tiny waist; thick, firm thighs; and sturdy legs. She was carefree, running to greet chilly Pacific Ocean waves. A feeling unlike any before rushed him, reminding him of holidays spent in Alabama sitting at his Grandma Imogene's table eating ambrosia. The citrusy sweetness of mandarin oranges and coconut flakes triggered endorphins—luscious heaven in a bowl that he just could not get enough of. He imagined Madeline in the same light. She was too sweet to get caught in the web of his crazy world. He was an athlete, a division one All-American superstar. With that came attention from the press, NBA prospects, and women. Game after game, uninhibited crops of them waited in the lobby of team hotels, bold enough to make it to the team's floor, and in some cases, inside the room. He quickly erased the thought. Madeline was off-limits—his best friend's first cousin, he certainly didn't want to cross that line.

His best friend Caleb told him she was valedictorian of her senior class with a full scholarship to Juilliard. Pretty, fine, and smart. She was into classical music. Not really his thing—reminded him of elevator music. Too stuffy, designed for an audience of formal, highbrow types. When he was eleven, he took piano lessons, albeit for six months. He knew just enough and had an ear for music that he could play without reading a single note. When he shared that information, he noticed her amber-colored eyes sparkle in the Malibu sunset. They had music in common. In her eyes, he wasn't JB, the All-American, collegiate all-team superstar, he was a friend who needed her to make the music in his head make sense.

He wasn't trying to get too close. He was already in a relationship with a girl named Basha—its status changed with the seasons. He was never a one-woman guy, not with the smorgasbord of women at his disposal. Again, he wasn't trying to get too close. But she came over, the plan was to work on music, create a song, put a melody to the lyrics he kept in a black-and-white speckled composition notebook. He put on Prince's Purple Rain album, and the pulsating drum sounds produced by the LinnDrum machine in the intro of "The Beautiful Ones" delighted his ears. They stopped writing to enjoy play time in the swimming pool.

Minutes later, they were on the floor inside his parents' pool house, dripping wet and smelling like chlorine. Her legs were wrapped around his waist, her lips trembling, her heart beating so fast he felt it pounding underneath him.

God, please let her be on the pill. Please, God.

When he entered, she screamed. She tensed up before her body trembled, her breath quickened, her teeth clattered near his ear. She became Grandma Imogene's ambrosia. He couldn't get enough. The sweetness weakened him.

Damn, damn, damn you, Maddie.

And although he was with Basha, when they kissed, it was Madeline's lips he imagined kissing. She owned his mind. Each time he saw Basha's eyes, it was Madeline's amber-colored eyes he imagined gazing into. He filled up an entire composition notebook with lyrics about her from the way she walked to the taste of her nipples. He read somewhere that the body was God's holy temple. With that being the case, he took every opportunity to worship. He found heaven between her honey-butter thighs. In the height of passion, he called out to God. Of all the girls he'd been with and he'd seen his share of beautiful faces during ecstasy—none were as angelic as Madeline's.

He should've known something was up when Mrs. Mary, Caleb's mother who was also Madeline's aunt, invited him and his parents over for dinner. That's when Madeline's father hit him with a bombshell: Madeline was pregnant.

* * *

JB enters their split-level home from the garage, flicking on lights to illuminate the hallway. The first place he checked was their music studio in the basement. He notices the covers still on the black baby grand Steinway and a pair of Yamaha PSRSX700 keyboards. He ascends the stairs and rushes straight to their bedroom suite where he finds Madeline sprawled across their bed, still fully dressed, one heel dangling off her foot. The tone that indicates the phone is off the hook blares like a screaming parrot. JB puts the phone back on its base and crawls in bed to awaken her.

"Baby," he whispers before kissing behind her ear.

She stirs, she blinks, her eyes open and adjust, her hand reaches back to touch him. He takes her hand and gently kisses it. She turns to face him.

"Hey," she whispers, puckering her lips. They kiss, their lips locking, and mouths opening and closing echoes in the stillness of early morning.

"Now I see why I couldn't reach you," he says, referring to the phone being off the receiver.

"I talked to Judy and Melody. It was so sweet listening to her sing. Then somehow, we got disconnected, and when I tried calling her back, I kept getting a busy signal, so I kept calling. I called Aunt Mary; she tried calling them. Finally, she went over to check on them. She called back to tell me everything was okay, but then Aunt Mary and I got disconnected. Then I tried calling my cousin Cassandra. She never picked up. Then I called Gilda and Daddy. Daddy's been keeping me calm. I watched a little of the game, and I tried to stay awake."

"Shhhhh." He places a finger up to her lips before lavishing her with kisses. She lies still with her eyes closed. The other shoe falls off, hitting the marble with a plop. He gently removes her gown.

Before JB arrived, her body was tense and wearing down from lack of sleep. Now JB's lips and hands are awakening, rejuvenating, and stimulating. Anticipation sends a shiver up her spine. She runs delicate, magic fingers through his nest of curls, kneading—her touch is soothing.

Moments later a primal groan escapes JB's lips—a raw release of frustration. The weight of being on a losing team and relentless expectations—they all converge, threatening to drown him. Madeline holds him the way a child clings to the softness and comfort of a stuffed toy. She listens to his breaths gradually get back to normal. He's asleep within seconds. Now she's wide awake, feeling his weight slowly getting heavy on her.

"Baby." She taps him. "Baby."

"Yes."

"Can we talk?"

"I'm listening."

"Are you coming to L.A. with me?"

"Yes."

She feels his weight get heavier the more he relaxes.

"JB." She taps him again.

"What?"

"We need to talk."

He removes himself from between her thighs. He keeps a small stack of hand towels on the nightstand. He grabs two, one to wipe himself and one for her. Once he's finished, he spoons her naked body against his. Her skin feels like a satin pillow against his fingertips.

"I'm listening," he tells her.

"I've been invited to go on a European tour," Madeline tells him.

The room is silent.

"Hello?"

"Okay," he mumbles, half asleep.

"That's it? Just okay?" She sighs, then glances at the digital clock on the nightstand next to her side of the bed. It reads 3:16.

JB's now snoring.

"JB. Baby." She taps him.

"What?" he answers. Half asleep, his tone is irritable.

"How do you feel about me going on tour?" she asks.

"When?"

"Next month."

"What?"

"I know it's soon."

"How long will you be gone?"

"Five months," Madeline answers.

"Five months?" The news jolts him awake. "What about me and Melody?"

"I'll be back when the new season starts for you, and as far as Melody, she's coming with me," she tells him.

"Mom's not spending five months in Europe."

"And she doesn't have to. I'll hire a nanny."

"No, you won't. No freaking way am I allowing a stranger to care for our child."

"JB, there's a rigorous vetting process. I wouldn't hire just anyone."

"Nope. Not happening. How long have you been planning this?"

Madeline thinks about the lunches with Lynnwood. "About a year," she answers.

The room is silent again.

"Why haven't you mentioned this before?" he asks.

"I wasn't sure if I wanted to go because it meant being away from you and Melody."

Madeline sighs. "The tour will be an opportunity to get name recognition, and besides, touring is exciting, and the timing coincides with your off season. Maybe you can join me on a few dates."

"I'm not sure if I'll have an off season," he mumbles.

"Why?"

"I may be in Barcelona."

"Barcelona? What's there?"

"Olympic games. There's still two spots left on the basketball team."

"And if you get a spot and I'm in Europe, then where does that leave Melody?"

"You can forget about the nanny," JB says.

They are both silent for a beat before Madeline speaks, "You don't want me going on tour."

"Did I say that?"

"You don't have to."

"I understand you want to tour and become a household name, but you have other obligations that are just as important."

"I know, and I'm trying everything I can to balance and fulfill them."

Silence fills the room. "I forgot to ask about your game tonight," Madeline says.

"It's a wrap."

"I'm sorry. I know how much you want a championship."

"I won't get it playing in Jersey."

"Where would you go?"

"Chicago, Houston, maybe L.A."

"Houston? Daddy would really like that," Madeline says.

"You'd be down with moving back to Houston?" he asks.

"I don't know. What team is Caleb on? Can you be teammates with him again?"

"No way I'd go to Detroit."

"Are you not happy here?"

"No," he answers.

"What are you going to do about it?" Madeline asks.

The same question gets asked of him by his father, his agent, the New Jersey team organization, and ESPN.

Just *what are you going to do, JB?*

Three

Northbound on the 405 leaving John Wayne Airport is a parking lot. Partly cloudy skies in the land of Disney traverse with more urgency than the chauffeur-driven town car Madeline and JB occupy. Madeline notices a gray haze in the distance where smoke and clearer air meet.

"Can you turn on the radio?" JB asks the chauffeur.

Michael Jackson's "Remember the Time" comes in clearly over the car's speakers. Madeline takes JB's arm and wraps it around her.

"We'll be here a while," she says, closing her eyes.

JB sighs. Although he and Madeline had plush first-class seats on an MD-80, the four-and-a-half-hour flight from Newark to Denver was wearisome. From Denver they boarded a regional jet airplane to Orange County Santa Ana. The chauffeur takes an exit and drives through neighborhoods with the logic, *Some movement in the right direction is better than no movement.* Now they are on the 5. Traffic is heavy, but it moves faster than the 405.

When their vehicle approaches the Los Angeles city limits, the skies are dark. Some lights on the expressway are out, making it difficult for the chauffeur to see in certain areas, but he meanders, navigates, and detours, turning down the radio, concentrating and combing the street, unflinching. JB notices the gas is barely at a quarter of a tank. He looks outside and recognizes landmarks.

"Find the nearest gas station, and let's fill up," he tells the chauffeur.

"Crazy part is locating one without a line," the chauffeur answers.

Madeline's heart races. "We're not about to run out of gas, are we?"

Buildings along Crenshaw Boulevard are smoldering in the aftermath of the rioting. JB remembers the stories his father, James, told him about the Watts Riots of 1965. James was a year into the league, and he remembered it happened during the summer. Nearly thirty years later, JB never imagined he'd see the devastation of his beloved city to this extent. It looked and felt less like L.A. and more like the war-torn countries he saw on the eleven o'clock news. When the town car pulls up, the entrance to the neighborhood is blocked by police.

The chauffeur presses a button, and his electronic window eases down. The police officers are on guard, hands just inches from their Sig Sauer p320s.

"They are residents. Is there any way you can let us pass?" The chauffeur's tone is on the brink of pleading.

The officers talk among themselves. Their radios crackle with the voices of dispatchers communicating in radio lingo.

Two of the officers who are Black approach the car. Madeline's heart races, and her ears ring. Suddenly, it's hard for her to swallow. JB holds her hand, somehow sensing her sudden apprehension.

"Who are you transporting?" the officer closest to the driver's side, burly in stature, asks. His brown complexion glimmers from the night sky. "Can you slowly let down the window?"

The window eases down, and the officer's flashlight shines on Madeline and JB in the backseat.

"Anyone else inside the car besides the three of you?" the second officer asks.

"No," both the chauffeur and JB answer.

"You need to drop that Jersey team and come out here to L.A.," the first officer holding the flashlight says.

The second officer gives him a look like, *What are you talking about?*

"It's JB from the New Jersey team," he tells him.

The second officer, as if he needs confirmation, shines his flashlight on JB and Madeline.

"JB." He laughs. His facial expression softens.

"In living color," JB answers back.

"Dude, I got to ask." The first officer stands back. "Boxers or briefs?"

The question elicits a laugh from everyone, including a chuckle from Madeline. JB's the spokesperson for a popular men's underwear line. The national commercial campaign has almost everyone he comes across asking him that question.

"Let them pass." The first officer radios to the other officers barricading the entrance. "You folks have a good night."

An officer who remained near the entrance of the blockade moves his squad car and allows them to enter. Madeline squeezes JB's hand. The neighborhood appears still intact; the streetlights still shine. Judy and James' house sits on one of the highest points of the neighborhood. JB and Madeline both feel relieved when the chauffeur pulls into the driveway. He gets out of the car to open their doors before opening the trunk to retrieve their luggage. The stench of rioting—burning rubbish—is in the air. JB opens his wallet and pulls out three crisp one-hundred-dollar bills.

"My wife and I thank you." JB places the bills in his palm. "So glad you didn't refuse us like all the others. Do you have a business card?"

The chauffeur grabs his wallet from his hip pocket, opens it up and retrieves a business card.

JB reads, *Valor Limo, owner Bo Young*.

"Thank you, Mr. Young."

"Call me Bo." They shake hands before Bo gets behind the wheel of the town car and coasts out of the driveway.

"Thank you, God," Madeline says once JB unlocks the front door and they are inside.

Judy walks out of the kitchen with Melody. The sight of Melody, with her hair brushed into a curly bun wearing a nightgown and duck house slippers, brings a warm flood of emotions over both Madeline and JB. The tears pour when Madeline and JB take their daughter into their arms, showering her with kisses. Her skin smells of Johnson's baby lotion, her hair smells like Judy washed it with strawberries.

Judy gets a hug and kiss from JB and Madeline.

"I honestly didn't think you two were going to make it," Judy says before taking a seat on the sofa across from them.

"We were getting here by any means necessary." Madeline kisses and nuzzles with Melody. She notices Melody's nails are painted bubble gum pink.

"Cops had the entrance blocked. Once upon a time, 'open sesame' used to be the catchphrase. Nowadays it's 'boxers or briefs.'" JB mimics the gesture he uses in the television commercial, where he stands with his hands by his sides. He looks into the camera, nods, flashes a smile and glances away.

"Why do you say that?" Judy asks.

"If I'd been anybody else, they wouldn't have allowed us to enter," he tells her.

"Celebrity has its advantage," Judy notes.

JB opens the sliding door that leads to the pool. Smitty, the family's Ibizan Hound is there to jump him. His tail wags at great speed. Kneeling to pet the dog, he looks out at the haze in the night sky. L.A. nights are magical when the view is clear and the lights dance and twinkle. Tonight, the atmosphere is weighty. Sirens wail in the distance. Most of the heavy action is south of him, the hardest hit area being South Central Los Angeles. A chopper's blades roar overhead with its spotlight behaving like a watchful eye over the region. He looks and sees Madeline and Melody walking in his direction. Smitty pants, licks Melody's face, and she waves him off.

"No." Melody tells the dog in a loud, distinct voice.

JB takes Melody's hand, and together with Madeline, they walk to the edge of the yard.

"At least the neighborhood is safe," Madeline says to him.

"I had a feeling it would be," JB replies.

Tear gas explosions and thundering chopper blades sound off in the distance. Melody points to the sky at another passing chopper.

"Look," she speaks.

"Yes. They are everywhere," he tells her, looking into her eyes, which are the color and shape of his and Judy's, his Filipina mother.

The air continues to brim with the stench of burned firewood. "Take her back inside," JB says. "I don't want her breathing this."

"Maybe you should come in too," Madeline says.

"I will shortly," he says before watching her and Melody walk back inside with Smitty trailing them. Standing alone, his mind drifted to the moment he returned home from the 1988 Olympic games in Seoul. He had been away from Madeline, who, at the time, had been his wife of just seven months. Melody was only four months old. When he opened the door and saw the adoring look in Madeline's eyes welcoming him home, uncontrollable tears flowed. Fans may have booed, the press may have scrutinized, but the loving energy he received from his new bride was unparalleled.

"Good. You made it," his father calls from the entrance.

James stood six-eight, walking with the gait of having two major knee surgeries.

He looks out at the haze swallowing the city. It covers the lights below like a tattered blanket.

They greet each other.

"What happened the other night?" James asks, referring to JB's team losing to the Cleveland team.

"They wanted it more than we did," JB answers.

"Your four years in Jersey flew by like a jet."

"Thanks for the reminder."

"Any idea what they're offering for you to stay?" James asks.

"Won't know until next week."

"What's the latest with Barcelona?"

"Still a couple of spots open. Won't know anything about that for at least a week or two."

"Barcelona will be an opportunity to redeem yourself," James tells him.

"Let's hope so. The '88 games put me in a foul mood."

"You got guys out here trying to decide between boxers or briefs," James says. Judy must've informed him about the exchange with the police.

"The campaign is going really well."

"I'm sure it is."

They are quiet for a brief five seconds.

"There's property I want in Alabama, not far from the home place," James says.

"What's the asking price?" JB asks.

"Forty-five thousand."

"How many acres?"

"Nine. Imagine land equivalent to seven city blocks, seven football fields, eighteen basketball courts."

"What do you plan to do?"

"Build a subdivision and provide affordable housing for first-time homeowners."

It's the latest in a string of investments that involves his father and others who've come to see him as the Bank of JB. An uncle approached him asking for a down payment on a building to open a soul food restaurant. Another relative asked if he could pay her tuition to cosmetology school. A relative in the Philippines needed money for house repairs. Fans write him letters asking for help paying their mortgages and credit card debts. His monthly payroll expenses include a percentage to his agent, his accountant, and Anna Palermo, a publicist and friend he's known since college. He and Madeline started Delightful, an endowment fund aimed at providing talented youth from low-income areas an opportunity to take music, dance, and acting lessons. JB never forgot how much sponsorship meant as a kid playing AAU basketball, so he sponsors a team of youth in L.A. and in New Jersey. There's a mortgage on the home in New Jersey and nearly two grand spent on rent for an apartment near the Juilliard campus. Not to mention a part-time cleaning staff for the home in New Jersey and the apartment in the city.

"This'll be the third piece of investment property. What's happening with Gulf Shores and Panama Beach?" JB asks.

"I plan to build a beach house on each one and rent them out," James says.

JB is silent.

"I know that look," James says. "What's up?"

"I need a drink," JB says.

"Sounds serious." James eyes him and beckons JB to follow him to the pool house. Inside, a wet bar is stocked with bottles of scotch, bourbon, brandy, and vodka. James pours vodka shots. He and JB down three.

"One more shot?" James asks.

"No." JB beats his chest with a fist, feeling the taste of the vodka ease its way down.

"What is that look about?" James asks. His eyes follow JB as he sits on a stool at the wet bar.

"Life since being in the league, not to mention going into it already married with a kid." JB answers.

"I know it's tough," James answers.

JB fingers the rim of his shot glass. His eyes flit as he gathers his thoughts. "Chicago is knocking."

"Chicago?" James looks startled. "They already have a solid team built around a franchise player. I don't understand why they're knocking."

"Could be a number of reasons."

"Why would you bounce?"

"Because winning means more to me than money." He looks his father square in the eyes.

"I understand you want to win. Winning is a drug. There's a high you get. Once you experience it, you want it repeatedly."

"It's a carrot that I've been chasing. I'm suited up, averaging over thirty minutes a game—all the wear and tear I'm putting on my body plus working with teammates who don't care. I've had enough. I want to win."

"My advice?" James begins.

JB's eyes are steady on the empty shot glass. A myriad of thoughts race as he toys with it.

"Stay in Jersey and strengthen your team. You are the nucleus. The smartest thing the organization can do is build the team around you," James tells him.

"Not the advice I wanted to hear, but in the spirit of sportsmanship and being a team player, sacrifice is forgoing the 'I' so that the 'we' succeed." JB's tone is jaded.

"When is the next time you see your agent?" James asks.

"Soon."

"Is this causing you the gray I'm seeing?" James jokes before examining the curls crowning JB's high-top fade.

JB runs a hand through his hair. "This league life's not for the faint of heart."

"Imagine how it was twenty-five, thirty years ago."

If JB had a dollar each time his father compared their league situations, there would be stacks of bills from the floor to the ceiling.

"Things good with the wife?" James asks.

"Her music keeps her busy. She told me after graduation she was going on tour. Said she'd be gone for five months."

"What? You're okay with that?" James asks.

"Hell no."

"I suppose she'll need Judy to come along to help with Melody."

JB is silent for a brief second. "She mentioned hiring a nanny, but I don't want a stranger caring for my daughter."

"One time, Melody asked me and Judy, 'Why are Mommy and Daddy always gone?' She's only four, but she understands Mommy and Daddy are out of the picture."

JB shakes his head. "I never want her to feel like we've abandoned her, like she's not important to us."

"I just hope Maddie accomplishes what she wants from this music business before Melody gets older. She keeps working, and Melody sees less of her. She'll grow up resenting her."

"As much as you were on the road when I was growing up, I never resented you," JB tells his father.

"But at least your mother was there. We can't say the same for Melody."

"If I stop Maddie from doing what she wants, then I'm the bad guy. Making music is her life. It allows her to step out of my shadow and not be consumed with my crazy-ass world."

"That classical music she performs, I imagine it doesn't bring a third of the amount of money you make."

JB just nods and listens.

"From the time Melody was born, Judy and I have put aside our lives to care for her so you and Maddie can have peace of mind and Maddie can accomplish her goal of finishing Juilliard. Now you and her need a serious talk about priorities. You best get a tighter rein on your household. Before you know it, you'll be fighting in court."

Four

It's the second day of May—the fourth day since the riots erupted—and the cries of police sirens still wail in the distance. The air still reeks with the stench of burnt rubbish. Madeline was restless throughout the night, awakening in intervals. She held Melody close, and hearing her breathing was soothing like a lullaby, which eventually calmed her to sleep.

Now she's awake, and the fresh, clean scent of bubble bath fills her senses. It's a scent reminiscent of Christmas mornings back home in Houston unwrapping and opening the box to see a brand-new baby doll and the brand-new smell. Madeline takes a moment to watch her daughter sleep. She is a living, breathing doll, complete with a cherub face and a honey-buttered complexion, like Madeline's. Her hair, a crown of deep brown curly ringlets, is loose. Madeline places her cheek next to the soft texture of Melody's cheek and closes her eyes. Too bad she isn't always there to soothe her aching cries. She holds her close until time stirs Melody awake.

***

Judy is at the stove when Madeline enters with Melody. James sits at the table reading the paper and sipping coffee. When Judy stayed at JB and Madeline's home in New Jersey to help with Melody, she prepared Filipino dishes for breakfast—tapsilog with garlic rice and eggs, sunny side up. Her champorado, a homemade porridge with chocolate, was a hit on the rare days Madeline was home and wasn't braving the chilly New Jersey winters.

This morning, it's American—lean turkey bacon, scrambled eggs whites, and whole wheat toast with cantaloupe slices.

"Please, Mommy, I don't want eggs and bacon, I want Apple Jacks," Melody tells her.

"But Melody, your grandmother just cooked this delicious breakfast."

"She loves her Apple Jacks," Judy says. "It's the only time she's allowed to have a little sugar."

Madeline pours a small bowl of Apple Jacks cereal to give Melody who eagerly anticipates it.

JB enters sporting a ribbed white shirt, jogging pants, and shower slippers. His hair is wet and curls distinct. A gold chain necklace hangs around his neck. Its links rest atop the outline of taut pecs. He greets Madeline, Melody, and Judy with a kiss before giving James a playful shove to the back of the head.

"Why didn't you come to bed?" Madeline asks JB as she butters her toast.

"I was chopping it up with Pops in the pool house." JB retrieves a plate from his mother.

"It wasn't long before I was talking to myself," James says with his nose still in the newspaper.

"The flight and the drive here wore me out. Pops threw a blanket over me." After preparing his plate, he sits next to Madeline, leans in and whispers, "You missed me?"

Madeline tries not to blush. Though James is still reading his newspaper and Judy is busy at the stove, Madeline's expressive and seductive eyes indicate *Yes, I missed you.*

He glances at his parents who are each still immersed in their activities before he leans and whispers to Madeline, "I just showered, but I don't mind taking another one."

"I'll keep that in mind," she whispers back. She turns her attention to Melody who's singing and amusing herself, using her spoon to push the O's in her bowl of Apple Jacks. Melody's high-pitched voice is sweet like the taste of ripened cherries.

"She loves to sing just like you," Madeline tells JB.

"Lolo says I'm a good singer." Melody joins in the conversation.

"Sing something for us," JB says to Melody.

"Like what?" Melody asks.

"Sing the song you sang to me the other night," Madeline tells her

"What song was that?" Melody asks.

"You don't remember?"

"Oh," she says before she proceeds to sing the song.

Madeline and JB are beaming along with JB's parents. Joy fills Madeline's heart at the innocence of the moment. Outside, L.A. crumbles around them, while inside is safe and comfortable as the four-year-old sings about love. They applaud when she finishes.

Judy, with a plate of food in hand, joins everyone sitting at the table. "I think I'll make lumpia later. Is that still on your diet?" she asks JB.

"It is today." He's emphatic before biting a slice of turkey bacon.

"I know you didn't go running with all the junk in the air," Judy says.

"Are you kidding?" JB shakes his head. "No running today. I'm bombarded with phone interviews."

James folds his newspaper and sets it aside. "Speaking of interviews, I have secured a big one."

"What is it?" JB and Judy ask.

"You might be looking at the next assistant coach for Cal State Long Beach," James replies.

"Cool, Pops. When's the interview?" JB asks.

"Monday," James answers.

"Wish we could hang around to celebrate with you, but Maddie and I leave tomorrow morning."

Madeline looks at Judy. "I still have classes on Monday, and I've got to prepare for graduation in two weeks."

Judy nods. "Can't come soon enough, huh?"

"I'm marking off the days on my calendar."

"Madeline, JB tells me you're going on tour," James says before taking a sip of coffee.

Madeline nods. "Yes."

"When is it, and how long will you be gone?" Judy asks.

"Starts next month. It'll last five months."

Judy's eyes flit as she takes in the information. "Wow. Five months." She looks at Melody.

"It's a major task, I understand. JB and I talked about it. I want to bring Melody with me, but I will also need a nanny to watch her."

"And that's where we clash," JB says.

Judy spent six months living with Madeline and JB in New Jersey while Madeline attended Juilliard and JB was in his rookie year in the NBA. That winter was harsh and the skies too dreary and gray for a Californian with tropical roots from Manila. She attended JB's games, and the fans made her blood boil with their loud and incessant comments and boisterous demeanor. On the rare occasion when the colors of the city popped like a picture-perfect postcard, she took Melody to Central Park. It was the place to be and a gathering place for au pairs and nannies.

As talkative as Judy is, as easy as it is for her to make new friends, East Coast living proved daunting. Not to mention her then twenty-one-year-old son and his new eighteen-year-old bride were still in their honeymoon phase. On one occasion, she arrived with Melody in tow after spending an afternoon in the city, elated to see JB and Madeline's vehicles parked out front. She searched almost every room in the house, except the basement where the music studio was. When she opened the door, she closed it immediately. JB and Madeline were deep in the throes of lovemaking, Madeline's impassioned cries pierced the air.

On another occasion, Judy awakened out of a deep sleep, and while still in a stupor, decided to go downstairs to the kitchen to grab a late-night snack. That's when she saw in the hazy, midnight gloom, her son pounding away. He had Madeline bent over the kitchen sink, their bodies clapped, their breaths quickened with each thrust. They needed privacy, and besides, she missed California. She got on a plane and headed back west, taking one-year-old Melody with her.

"I would love it if you and James could accompany me on some of the dates," Madeline says. She notices Judy and James exchange glances.

"Where will you be touring?" Judy asks.

"I have dates in London, Paris, Rome, Geneva, Berlin..." Madeline smiles after announcing each city.

"If you're taking Melody with you, who's going to watch her on the dates we can't make it?" James asks.

"Have you thought about that?" JB asks her.

"You will watch her," is Madeline's response to him.

"I'll be in Barcelona. Did you forget?" JB adds.

"Why?" Judy asks.

"What do you mean why?" JB gives her a look.

"Oh, yes, the Olympic games." Judy gets excited. "You got selected?"

"Not yet."

"They'll pick you," she says, forking her egg whites.

Madeline turns her attention back to Melody, and all that's left of her cereal is a bowl of strawberry-colored milk. "I'm done," Melody declares with a smile. "May I be excused? I want to watch Barney."

Madeline wipes the corners of her mouth with a napkin before placing it over her half-eaten plate, "Can I watch Barney with you?" she asks.

"Yes." Melody's eyes light up. "Come on." She grabs her mother's hand. For a four-year-old, she has a firm grip.

"Remember what I said earlier," JB calls out, winking.

Madeline playfully rolls her eyes, following Melody down the hallway to her room. Once inside, Melody finds the VHS tape and inserts it inside a VCR. Madeline is impressed she already knows how to use it. They sit and watch a purple dinosaur named Barney and his friends sing songs about what they want to be when they grow up. Madeline watches Melody dance along with the video of the dinosaur naming a job for each letter of the alphabet. Soon they're playing with her collection of Barbie dolls.

"I like playing with them," she tells Madeline.

"Me too," Madeline gushes.

"Guess what? Lola likes dolls, too," Melody says, referring to her grandmother.

They now play with another collection of baby dolls, arranging them at a table to have a tea party.

"*Ummm.* This is delicious," Madeline says, holding a saucer and sipping from a teacup.

Melody gives some of her imaginary tea to one of the dolls. The door opens, and JB appears.

"You can't start a party without me," he says, stepping over scattered Barbies and baby dolls and finding a seat on the floor next to Madeline. She gives him a teacup and saucer.

"Miss Melody, would you please pour your daddy a cup of tea?"

Melody pretends she's pouring tea.

"Thank you," JB says once he receives it. He puts the cup close to his nose. "I can tell this is going to be good."

"Be careful. It's too hot," Melody says, and it sounds like something she may have heard Judy say to her during their tea party time.

JB and Madeline sip imaginary tea from their cups.

"Good. Just like I knew it would be," JB says to Melody.

Madeline agrees.

"Hey, where's the food?" JB asks Melody. "We can't have a tea party without food."

Melody opens his hand and pretends she's putting something in his palm. She does the same to Madeline.

"What is it?" JB asks.

"Food," she responds.

"What kind of food?" Madeline asks.

Melody shrugs.

"I know. Let's pretend we're having tea cake and cucumber sandwiches," Madeline suggests.

"Okay," Melody cheerfully agrees.

"Tea cake. Wow. You went back to Texas," JB says.

"One of my fondest memories of my mother is that she loved to host tea parties in our home, and I distinctly remember the smell of butter and vanilla from those tea cakes." Madeline's expression is reflective. "The only person I know who comes close to baking a delightful batch is Aunt Teal. Too bad she's back in New Orleans."

"I bet if you gave Moms the recipe, she could do it."

"I know. Judy is incredible like that." Madeline watches Melody talk to her dolls.

"She thinks you're pretty incredible, too," JB says.

Madeline turns to glance at her husband.

"And so do I," he adds, gazing into her eyes. The magnetic energy he brings still gives her butterflies, reminiscent of the summer of 1987, when she began to see him differently than she did prior to that. They want to kiss each other, long and deep, but Melody is there.

"What are you doing?" Melody asks.

JB and Madeline laugh. "Daddy and I are giving each other sweet eyes."

"What's that?" Melody asks. She holds up her doll, imitating her parents.

"Now you're giving your dolly sweet eyes," Madeline says.

"Too funny, Melody." JB takes her hand and brings her close for a hug. "Daddy and Mommy love you so much," he tells her.

She nods like she understands.

"Even when we're not here, we still love you," Madeline tells her.

"Okay. Bye." She makes a quick dash out of the room. Her feet pitter-patter down the hallway.

"Melody?" JB and Madeline call out.

"Guess she's had enough of us," JB says before sipping his imaginary tea.

Madeline sips her imaginary tea.

"Let's make up for last night," JB tells her. "I have an hour and a half before my first call."

"Not in here."

"Hell no. The pool house like we used to. They won't hear you."

***

Madeline's aunt, Dr. Mary May Honoré greets her and Melody at the door after JB drops them off. Seeing Aunt Mary suddenly makes her emotional. Aunt Mary holds her close.

"There," she says in her low, raspy voice. "We're okay. Your Uncle Frenchy is resting upstairs."

Madeline gives her a care package. "Courtesy of Judy."

"I love it. Hello, lovely." She kneels to give Melody a peck on the cheek. "Come inside."

Madeline and Melody find a spot on the sofa. Memories of summers past and the familiar scent of polished hardwood floors recall a time when life was simpler.

"Our housekeeper lives in Vermont Square, and that happens to be one of the areas affected by the rioting. We told her she could stay with us, but she insists on staying home. Judy and I talked on the phone yesterday, and I casually mentioned Pancit."

Aunt Mary takes the package into the kitchen. "Care to join me? This dish smells divine."

Madeline removes a coloring book and a box of crayons from the satchel that contains her sheet music—about four years' worth of compositions that she keeps guarded. Melody takes the coloring book and crayons and sits on the floor. Madeline sits at a bar stool. Aunt Mary dishes up a plate for Madeline and herself.

"No thanks. It's for you and Uncle Frenchy," Madeline tells her.

"What about Melody?" Aunt Mary asks.

"She's fine." Madeline glances at Melody sitting on the floor singing and coloring.

Aunt Mary takes a bite of her dish. Her expression is blissful. "Your mother-in-law is heaven sent. She never disappoints."

"Never, without a doubt. When's the last time you talked to Aunt Teal?" Madeline asks.

"Last week. Frenchy and I were in New Orleans for Jazz Fest."

"I miss her."

"Believe me, we all do." Aunt Mary pours a glass of Chardonnay. "Enjoy a glass with me."

"No thanks."

"It's madness what's happening right now," Aunt Mary says.

"I just hope JB and I get out of here tomorrow."

"You mean out of LAX?"

"Yes. The eight o'clock flight."

"You'll be on the flight with Frenchy. He's flying into Newark to see Caleb play at Madison Square Garden against the New York City team."

"Is he flying the plane?"

"No. Just a regular passenger."

"JB's bummed his team is out of the running."

"It's do or die for Caleb tomorrow night, or he'll be having an early summer like JB."

"How is Caleb?" Madeline asks, referring to her cousin.

"He called earlier today. He watched the news, and of course he was worried. I assured him we are safe."

"And Cassandra?" she said, referring to her other cousin. "I really wish I could make it to her graduation next week."

"She'll understand." Aunt Mary twirls more noodles around her fork.

"My schedule is hectic. I hardly get an opportunity to connect. How is she doing in flight school?"

"Cassandra just got her private pilot's license."

"That is beyond cool."

"Fifteen hundred hours, and she'll have her commercial pilot's license."

"Aunty, that's impressive. Have you been in flight with her?"

"I have. She's an astute flier. Of course it comes naturally. Since she could walk, she's been in airplanes with her father."

"And how is Rosie?" Madeline asks, referring to Aunt Mary's adoptive daughter.

"This fall she'll start her second year at USC. I'm so proud of her. I'm proud of all of you."

"Thank you. It wasn't easy." Madeline sighs.

Aunt Mary chews silently. "I commend you."

Madeline rests her chin inside her hand. "Are you considering opening another youth outreach center?" she asks.

Aunt Mary once operated a youth outreach center in one of the roughest neighborhoods in Los Angeles. It operated for ten years until a violent incident involving one of the youths caused it to close its doors.

"No. Gun violence is still a thing around these parts." Aunt Mary responds.

"That's unfortunate, Aunty."

"I've come up with new, innovative ways to outreach. I take my self-awareness message to different high schools, and so far, it's working."

"Do you still keep in touch with some of your eaglets from the youth center?"

"Damon. He's doing tremendously well, given the circumstances."

"Wow." Madeline's mind drifts back to the horrific scene she witnessed five years ago at Aunt Mary's youth outreach center. Damon was lying on the ground, his leg covered in a pool of blood. A victim of random gun violence.

"What are you thinking?" Aunt Mary asks.

"Where do I begin?" Madeline chuckles. "Has Cassandra had any issues? I remember after the incident you had us see a doctor."

"She's managed to compartmentalize the trauma. It hasn't affected her ability to fly a plane."

"I have recurring dreams about it."

"Care to describe them?"

"There's blood everywhere and children screaming and gunfire."

"Dreams are common," Aunt Mary responds.

"I guess I've learned to compartmentalize it, too."

"How is married life? Is it everything you imagined?" Aunt Mary asks.

"It is for the most part, although my mind wonders sometimes when he's on the road," Madeline admits.

"It's not uncommon. I still wonder about your uncle," Aunt Mary replies, "but I've also taken into consideration what I'm dealing with."

"I want to trust JB."

Aunt Mary wipes each corner of her mouth. "I am a firm believer, whatever is done in secrecy, over time, will eventually manifest itself."

"Has Uncle Frenchy cheated on you?" Madeline feels the hairs on her arm stand. She regrets asking the first question that pops into her head, but for the same reason is fearful of Aunt Mary's response.

Aunt Mary, with glass in hand, takes a moment before answering. "There was an incident with a flight attendant. I guess his conscience must've gotten the best of him because he confessed."

Madeline's heart pounds, her cheeks and skin flush with the revelatory news.

"How long ago was that?" she asks.

"Right after I opened the youth center. He said I spent too much time there, and I had little for him." She waves her hand. "I call BS. When it comes to infidelity, there's no justification."

"Was that the only time he cheated?" Madeline asks.

"No, sweetheart. After your mother passed away in 1982 and my mother, your Grandmother Magdalene, passed away in 1984, I went through a period of low-grade depression. As much as I wanted to be present and beneficial to Frenchy's needs, the will just wasn't there. I began to see less of him, and I had my suspicions he was cheating again."

"Same flight attendant?" Madeline asks.

"No. This home wrecker was once an associate of mine. She was originally from Hawaii."

Madeline's eyes ballooned upon hearing that.

"*Home wrecker* is the nicest word I can use to describe her," Aunt Mary replies.

"You knew this person?" Madeline asks.

"Yes. She's been to our home. A brazen cow."

Madeline listens, on the edge of her seat.

"Frenchy flies 747 jets, long hauls all over Asia—Shanghai, Tokyo, Taipei, Beijing, you name it. I noticed he was flying to Honolulu. Mind you he used to say Hawaiian trips weren't worth the time and effort it took to get to the airport. Yet, he was flying there quite often."

"What did you do?" Madeline asks. She listens intently to every word.

"I booked myself on a flight. I found out about the hotel where the crew was staying. I deplaned, got to the hotel, sat in the lobby, and waited. When your uncle saw me, he didn't know whether to scratch his watch or wind his butt."

"Oh dear, Aunty. What did you do next?"

"My charm school etiquette was this close—" She measures inches with her fingers—"to going out the window. How dare they frolic like they haven't a care in the world."

Madeline's skin is flushed as she imagines the scene playing out the way Aunt Mary describes it. "What did he do to make it right?"

"Marriage counseling and lots of soul searching. It takes years to build back trust once it's compromised."

"Wow, Aunty. I wouldn't have imagined this. I mean you and Uncle Frenchy seem to have it together." Madeline feels a tap, and Melody's at her side.

"May I swim in the swimming pool, please, Mommy?" she asks.

"Now is not a good time," Madeline tells her. "Why don't you finish coloring?"

Melody mopes back to her spot on the floor and resumes.

"She's going to want a playmate soon," Aunt Mary says before taking a sip.

Madeline quickly waves off the notion of having another child. "What were we talking about?" she asks.

"We were talking about trust," Aunt Mary responds. "I've noticed where there's pilots, pro athletes and preachers commingled with power and prestige, there's bound to be problems." She leans into Madeline and lowers her voice, "Not to mention pounds of pussy and pissloads of pain."

Madeline covers her mouth, tickled by Aunt Mary's candidness.

Madeline was no stranger to candid conversation regarding husbands and infidelity. She became acquaintances with JB's teammates' wives and girlfriends, sometimes meeting with them for lunch. On occasion, when she attended his games, she met with a couple of the wives.

"*When you won't, there's someone else who will,*" she recalls one of them telling her. They loved giving unsolicited advice on what it took to keep the fire burning.

Madeline always remembered what JB told her, "Never discuss our private lives with anyone."

"A woman with white wine will eventually speak her sober mind," Aunt Mary begins. "But I've always felt that I was at fault when you got pregnant."

"Stop, Aunt Mary." Madeline holds up her hand.

"Maddie, let me get this off my chest. Me not being around to watch you, me not paying attention to the signs. That put into motion you having to get married at eighteen, which I was never in favor of. I still believe JB only married you because if he hadn't, he was going to jail."

"Aunty, he was willing to risk losing it all for me."

"Earlier you expressed doubt. Some insecurity. What gives?" In that instant, Aunt Mary's eyes remind Madeline of her deceased mother's. They are full of worry and concern.

"Like Uncle Frenchy, JB is on the road, and there are women in every city trying for an opportunity to be with him."

"Prayer," Aunt Mary states. "Lots of prayer, that's the only way you'll get the final P word of the day."

"And what's that?"

"Peace," Aunt Mary answers before finishing her glass of Chardonnay.

"Thank you," Madeline says while in the back of her mind she wonders if those urges of JB's persist on the road.

Five

JB opens the front door to see Frances "Frenchy" Honoré, Madeline's uncle, and his best friend Caleb's father. They greet each other with a secret handshake, signifying their membership in the same fraternity. JB has his and Madeline's suitcases packed and ready to go by the front door.

"You had breakfast?"

JB invites him inside. He follows JB to the kitchen where Madeline, Judy, James, and Melody are.

"Good morning, everyone. Wow. It smells good here. Hmmm. It's been a while since I smelled a home-cooked meal." He sits next to Madeline at the table.

Chuckling, James sets down his newspaper to remove his reading glasses and wipes his eyes. "Mary starving you again?"

"I tell you, that Pancit dish Judy sent by Madeline was manna from heaven."

"I have a care package of lumpia for you to take on the flight," Judy tells Frenchy.

"Bless you," Frenchy says. "J, sure you wouldn't mind a wife swap?" Frenchy jokes.

Judy pours Frenchy a cup of coffee. The remark is benign to James who only chuckles.

"We've been catching hell since the riots broke out. My wife acts like she doesn't know her way around the kitchen," Frenchy explains.

"You're a good cook, Frenchy," Judy says.

"True, but after sixteen hours on a plane, the last thing I want to do is come home and cook." Frenchy sips from his cup of coffee.

Judy offers him breakfast.

"I'm too well raised to refuse," Frenchy answers. He smiles at Melody. "Hello, little niece."

"Mary's not attending the game with you?" Judy asks Frenchy.

"No" is his response, as Judy places a plate of hot Filipino breakfast tortas in front of him. "Thank you," he tells her.

"These are phenomenal," JB says to him.

"I already know" is his response.

JB sits across from them. "I haven't had an opportunity to talk to Floyd," he tells Frenchy, referring to his best friend Caleb, using the nickname given when he pledged undergrad.

"Neither have I," Frenchy says before taking a bite.

"In the league, everything happens at lightning speed. Before you know it, you're out and watching it on television like everyone else," JB says, his tone soft and laced with regret.

Caleb's team was still alive, and that meant another opportunity for a shot at the championship and bragging rights.

"Brother, there's always next season," Frenchy tells him. "Speaking of which, I read an article in *Sports World Magazine* about you becoming a free agent."

"I told Pops I'll take a solid, cohesive team any day," JB responds.

"Wouldn't it be something to see you in a Los Angeles team uniform?" Frenchy asks.

JB smiles and glances at his father. "My roots. We'll wait and see what happens."

He notices Madeline has been quiet for some time. Perhaps she is still thinking about last night. When she returned from visiting

Aunt Mary, she entered the pool house to find JB lounging on the sofa bed talking on a cordless phone. His eyes were closed and his voice lower than usual. His right hand was inside his shorts, and he quickly removed it and sat up—startled to see her. He ended the conversation with the person on the other line and sat there quietly gauging her reaction while Jodeci's "Come and Talk to Me" played softly in the background.

"Who was that?" she asked.

"Lilly," he answered.

"Lilly?" Madeline remembered Lilly. She was an actress, someone JB dated once. They'd met, even hung out with Lilly and Benny, the man who would eventually become Lilly's husband, together at a nightclub and a piano bar. Madeline felt her blood simmer beneath the surface. "Why are you talking to her?"

"She reached out. Since The Show ended, she's been in the dumps, and from the looks of it, her marriage to Benny is headed in the same direction."

"She's calling you? What are you, her marriage counselor now?"

"Come here." He motioned.

"No." She stood with arms folded, "You looked comfortable, lying there, talking to her with your hand inside your shorts."

"Trust me, it's not what it looks like."

"Explain." She stood her ground, not moving.

He smiled and gave her a puppy-dog look. "Can we all get along?" He echoed Rodney King, the motorist beaten by four white police officers, who at a recent televised press conference asked that very question.

"I'm waiting," she continued.

"I know it looked hella disgusting, but the truth is, I was relaxing, listening, being a supportive friend, and I happened to be resting my hand inside my shorts. You startled me, not because I was doing anything wrong, but because you entered abruptly, which had me on guard."

"Sounds plausible." Madeline stood with arms folded.

"Come here." He extended his hand.

A sigh of trepidation escaped her lips.

He extended the other hand. "You're the only woman I want."

"Stop."

"I mean it," he said, looking directly into her eyes, which have always been one of her most extraordinary features. They were amber, the rarest of eye colors—a golden brown that radiated and sparkled. Looking into them wielded the power to cause an imposing six-foot-eight, 218-pound power forward to soften—become weak, weightless, helpless—like a baby. When she was unsure of whether she should believe him, she blinked constantly, and for someone so beautiful and so delicate, JB often fed her partial truths in teaspoon doses.

If she wanted to know how his day went, he replied, *"I'll be up front with you. Yes, I had to beat several women off with a stick, but nothing happened. Yes, some teammates and I went to a bar, had rounds of beer before we chilled in the champagne room."*

Mind you, Madeline's idea of a bar is a place like on the sitcom Cheers. Her idea of a champagne room is where men with refined tastes go to have champagne, cigars, and converse freely about sports, maybe certain aspects of religion—in her mind, her father could possibly find relaxation in a champagne room.

Did she need to know that for the past five months, Lilly's been crying on his shoulder? That one night, Lilly called him crying after discovering Benny was a serial cheater, and JB spent the evening comforting her and Lilly cried herself to sleep in his arms?

He saw Madeline relent, take his hand, and succumb to the spellbinding power he's had from the moment he first touched her.

Moments later, the room was pitch black. The CD changer in the stereo segued from R&B group Jodeci to R&B crooner Keith Washington's ballad, "Kissing You."

"You're the only one," he whispers in her ear.

He can't see the impassive expression in her eyes, but he senses it in her movements. She is going through the motions. Later that morning, he awakens to find himself in bed alone.

***

Madeline has Melody in her arms while JB loads their luggage in the trunk of Frenchy's Lexus. The sedan runs idle, with Frenchy patiently sitting behind the wheel.

"Mommy will call you as soon as I get there." She kisses her daughter's round cheeks, holding her cheek to cheek.

Melody makes eye contact with her father, her almond-shaped eyes full of questions. JB has already showered her with enough hugs and kisses. It's Madeline who's having the hardest time saying goodbye. Judy and James approach them.

"I'll see you in two weeks, I promise," Madeline says before watching her walk away. She stands between her grandparents and waves goodbye.

Once inside the car, Madeline sits in the backseat. JB slides in next to her. Together they wave until they no longer see his parents and Melody. At that point, a rush of emotions overtakes her, and Madeline sobs inconsolably. JB takes her hand, but her grasp is limp, not firm.

Frenchy is unusually quiet. Station KJLH normally plays the latest in R&B and adult contemporary music now has its phone lines open for people to call in and express themselves regarding the riots. Outside, the haze lingers, giving the skies a gray and gloomy appearance. JB takes Madeline's face into his hands and brings it closer for a kiss that she doesn't reciprocate. He tastes the salt from her tears as they fall upon his mouth.

She's still upset about last night. "What can I do to make it better," he whispers.

She shakes her head.

"Tell me."

She turns away.

A voice on the radio cries, "There were people injured because of the looting. The police were across the street watching it, and there was nothing they could do. It was already out of hand. People were going crazy, stepping all over each other."

Frenchy comes to a stop as a fleet of California national guard vehicles cross with troops onboard armed with assault rifles.

"Is this still America?" Frenchy shakes his head. "My God."

JB looks out the window. Buildings that were once viable storefronts are giant heaps of smoldering debris. Something in him feels guilty about leaving. Maybe once he sees where he stands with the New Jersey team and the Olympics, he will find time to come back to volunteer and help rebuild. Maybe.

Boarding the flight, JB and Madeline secure the last row of seats in business first class with Frenchy sitting across the aisle. Madeline hasn't spoken a word to JB since breakfast. A flight attendant—a vision in navy blue—tall, slender, brown complected with a neatly trimmed bob—approaches with a silver tray in hand.

"Oh my. You're JB," she gushes.

"No. He just looks like him." Frenchy winks.

"So happy to have you on our flight." She presents JB with a menu. Her smile is practiced, her eyes assessing. She's struck by his presence. It's a phenomenon he's become accustomed to. "Can I get you anything?" she purrs, her fingers brushing his shoulder.

"I'd like a menu for my wife," JB tells her.

"Oh. Absolutely," she says, handing a menu to Madeline, yet her eyes are fixed on his.

Madeline remains quiet. JB notices she hasn't said much to Frenchy either.

"Are you eating?" he asks Madeline.

Madeline's voice is ice. "No, thank you" is her reply before handing him the menu. He gives it back to the flight attendant, her smile now brittle.

"Enjoy your flight," she says, her gaze lingering on JB before moving down the aisle.

"Are you sure you're not eating? This is a five-hour flight," he reminds her.

"I'm not hungry. Besides, I'm not liking what she's serving."

JB chuckles. "I see. So, you'd rather starve than to have the flight attendant serve you up a delicious mouthwatering eight-ounce steak?"

Madeline is wearing her mother's oversized vintage sunglasses, her honey-complected skin still flush from crying is now seething. For the duration of their marriage, she's encountered numerous bold, flirtatious women. She tells herself, *Yes, JB's the sexiest, most desirable athlete on the planet, and it's me who's captured his heart. I'm the true north on his compass, but my insecurities still arise. Especially after what I saw last night in the pool house and how JB tries to downplay it—attention from women comes with the territory of being a famous professional athlete. Either I continue to deal with it or pray for that peace that Aunt Mary talked about.*

"I keep replaying the look on your face when I walked in and saw you lying there on the couch." Her voice is low and discreet.

"Baby, trust me. It was nothing."

He sees his reflection in her dark tints. Taking her hand, he kisses and holds it. "You know what I haven't heard you say to me in a long time?"

"What?"

"That you love me. You still love me?" JB's voice is a fragile thread—a plea. His vulnerability hangs in the air.

"Of course I love you," Madeline's hushed, delicate voice trembles.

The airplane cabin seems to hold its breath—the hum of the engines, the distant chatter of Frenchy's voice along with the other passengers.

JB removes her glasses, his gaze now bores into hers. He leans in, his lips touching hers. "Then you've got to trust me," he whispers.

Madeline nods. And as the airplane takes off down the runway and soars, the tension that was present earlier slowly drifts away.

For now.

Six

Monday morning, and six stories up inside the apartment on 56 West 65th Street, Madeline awakens alone in a king-sized bed. No matter how late the night gets, JB is up at dawn for his morning ritual, a run down the block westward through Central Park. Sheet music containing original compositions are stacked in a neat pile atop the nightstand on her side of the bed. She notices the blinking light on the answering machine and presses play. There are fourteen new messages.

The first message is marked Sunday, 6:03 p.m.: "Maddie, hope everyone is okay in L.A." It's her cousin, Gracie, the tone of her Brooklyn accent is soft and maternal in nature. "Call me today, or let's meet tomorrow morning for breakfast. Ciao."

The machine beeps and plays the next message, marked 2:38 p.m., also on Sunday. "Madeline, Lynnwood here." His rich New Orleans accent reminds her of Uncle Frenchy's creole drawl. "Listen, I'm looking over the music to your 'Sunset Composition.' I'm digging it, seriously. I want to open with it on the tour. Let's connect soon so we can get in some rehearsals with the orchestra. Later."

Madeline replays the message again. She pictures Lynnwood in the rehearsal chamber pouring over the sheet music, dissecting every note. When he attended one of her recitals with the chamber orchestra, she played the piece.

"I know a virtuosa when I hear one," he said to her after the performance. "I can tell by the tone and the usage of certain instruments."

She was impressed. He dissected and analyzed her composition with the skillset of a surgeon. He had a swagger about him from the Brooks Brothers suits he wore to his vast musical versatility.

The other twelve messages could wait.

* * *

Gracie always appears as if she just leaped from the pages of *Town & Country* magazine. She sees Madeline and gives her a hug. For this morning's breakfast, they both enjoy bagels with lox and cream cheese. Madeline likes adding capers for more flavor.

"I've got good news," Gracie begins. "I've been keeping this under wraps for quite some time because frankly, I didn't know if I was making the right decision."

"What about?" Madeline anticipates more.

"I'm going to Rome to perform with the Teatro dell'Opera. Their director was in town. He saw my recital. He came up to me afterward to express his appreciation of my amazing aria. They want to hire me."

"Gracie, that's wonderful."

"Isn't it?"

"It's what you've always wanted, right?" Madeline says before taking a small bite of her bagel. "When do you leave?"

"Next week."

"Next week?"

"Yes."

"We have classes next week."

"Listen, this is a once-in-a-lifetime shot for me."

"I don't understand," Madeline replies.

"I've met all my requirements; the rest of the classes are fillers."

"But you need those classes to graduate."

Gracie is silent.

"No, Gracie." Madeline senses where this is going.

"I was trying to find a way to ease this in, but—" Gracie's skin is flushed.

"You've come so far and worked so hard. Can't you hold off?"

"No."

"You're two weeks away from graduation."

"It's not a big deal for me if I don't attend the commencement. What's important is me taking this opportunity with Teatro dell'Opera."

Madeline is crushed. "Your parents are going to be so upset."

"My parents are on tour. They wouldn't have made it anyway."

"What about your grandmother?"

Gracie rolls her eyes at the mention of her grandmother.

Before Madeline arrived in New York, she believed Aunt Mary to be the last surviving offspring of PC May. Aunt Mary has an older sister, twenty-four years her senior, who resides in the hamlet of Chappaqua. Madeline met Aunt Charlotte during the Christmas break of her first year. When Gracie introduced her as PC and Magdalene's granddaughter, she was rendered speechless. She looked directly at Madeline, yet her eyes had a faraway expression. It took minutes before she finally warmed up to Madeline. When Madeline left, Gracie filled her in. It was rumored PC May was seeing Magdalene, Madeline's grandmother. He divorced so that he could marry Magdalene.

Madeline tosses the rest of her bagel, lox, and cream cheese with added capers. News of Gracie leaving just shy of graduation suppresses her appetite. She's seen it before: Many start out walking through Juilliard's doors, but few remain. Once they're presented with an opportunity, they're out the door.

As always, from the moment Madeline entered, the atmosphere at Juilliard brims with musicians, vocalists, actors, and dancers. She looks to the left to see a cellist playing Johann Sebastian Bach's "Prelude, Suite No. 1." Straight ahead, a svelte ballet dancer in leotard and leg warmers stretches at the barre. An actress' voice rings with thunder reciting Macbeth, "Tomorrow, tomorrow and tomorrow."

Madeline is still shaken by Gracie's announcement. Yet Gracie continues to her reserved practice room to work on her vocals. Madeline is in a practice room across the hall. She uses a metronome and starts out with finger warm ups, striking the keys with quick, light strokes. Within the hour, the Steinway in the practice room comes alive with Ravel and Debussy. At the end of the hour, she's off to a piano performance class. Usually, Gracie meets her between classes. Not this time. Her piano performance class is followed by a piano literature class and chamber music workshops, then lunch. Still, no Gracie.

Then she remembers a meeting scheduled with Lynnwood. It's late evening before she enters a practice hall inside the Lincoln Center. Lynnwood, prominent, sporting a navy Brooks Brothers suit, plays his trumpet with classical phrasing backed by a chamber orchestra of nearly fifty musicians. The tempo is allegro, cheerful, and bright. His expression is intense. His fingers tap the valves with finesse and dexterity. Madeline finds a seat and listens. She taps her foot along with the rhythm until Lynnwood signals the orchestra to stop.

"Right here is where the piece transcends to another dimension." Lynnwood notices Madeline sitting in the audience and takes a quick glance at his watch.

"One last time, from the top," he tells them, counting off before the orchestra proceeds to play the piece again. Once they finish, he invites Madeline to the stage where she sits in front of a piano and plays her "Sunset Composition" as Lynnwood and the orchestra listen. After she plays, he speaks to the other musicians.

"I wanted you all to hear the profound joy in the composition and hear from the composer her thoughts on this piece," he tells them.

Madeline thinks briefly about it. "My mother loved sunsets," she begins. "She did mission work, and I remember her recalling the prettiest sunsets were right off the coast of Ghana. The phenomenon of the colors in the sky suggests a melody very much like 'Clair de Lune' by Claude Debussy."

Madeline plays a portion of the song. "When I wrote it, I heard the opening chord shimmer like sun-kissed waves. I heard a cascade of arpeggios like the sun bidding farewell, casting its final rays." She demonstrates. "I heard strings with legato phrases and woodwinds like flutes, and clarinets."

The tone and volume of the piano crescendos before it ends in a delicate pianissimo. The way she plays the piece allows the notes to linger in the listener's ears like stardust. The song ends.

"Play it again, this time I want the orchestra to play." Lynnwood says.

He listens to the orchestra before he proceeds to blow his trumpet. He's versatile with the phrasing, shifting effortlessly from classical to jazz phrasings. Madeline didn't have a trumpet in mind when she wrote the composition. However, his trumpet did add a little more depth to the piece, but it is unsettling. Madeline stops playing. Everyone looks at her.

"Piano and orchestra, please," she tells him.

"You got a problem with my trumpet?" Lynnwood pretends he's offended. It gets a laugh from the musicians.

"I want to keep it close to the original composition."

"Why not consider it?" he says. "Let me bless this piece."

"Piano and orchestra, please," she tells him. *The nerve. If I wanted a trumpet as the lead instrument, I would've written it.*

"Piano and orchestra. proceed," he says and steps away without argument. Just an added smirk on his lips. Living in New York City for the past four years has taught Madeline several traits—among them assertiveness and standing one's ground, regardless of who it is.

An hour later, after rehearsals, he pulls her aside. "My apologies," he tells her.

She smiles. "You understand, as a composer." Though in that moment she wanted to voice her disapproval in a not-so-subtle way. She poured her heart into the piece. It was her love song and the instruments she chose best captured the essence of the composition.

"I get it, I get it." He holds up his hand. "Respect."

"I'm honored you want to include my piece in the lineup."

"It's a brilliant piece of music," he answers.

"I have hundreds more just waiting to see the light of day."

"You say that casually like you're talking about a pair of shoes." He chuckles, he's only thirty-one, but his eyes—deep pools of sepia—hold stories like they've witnessed smoky jazz clubs in New Orleans, where Louis Armstrong's trumpet wailed.

"When it comes to music, my brain doesn't seem to have an off switch," she tells him, referring to the number of compositions she's written.

He smiles with a nod, and there is an awkward moment of silence.

"Can we work more on this tomorrow?" Madeline asks.

"Sure, uh, our camps will link up and go over the last-minute details for the tour."

"I'm looking forward to Europe," she says.

"I've toured Europe. In fact, I dropped out of Juilliard and spent a year over there. I didn't want to come back."

The tour is for five months. Suppose she gets to Europe with Melody and doesn't want to leave; how will she manage to stay married?

"See you tomorrow," she tells Lynnwood and strolls out of Alice Tulley Hall and out to the plaza where the Metropolitan Opera House and Koch buildings are. It's nighttime, and the city is forever bustling with a pulse that never stops.

It's been a long time. Maybe I'll surprise my husband and cook dinner tonight, if only I can remember what's in the pantry.

She's immersed in her thoughts before she realizes she's already made it to the main entrance of the apartment building on West 65th Street. Across the street, watching Madeline walk inside, stands Basha, JB's ex-girlfriend.

Seven

Ablack-and-white movie poster of JB mid-flight preparing to dunk hangs prominent in a gallery along with other framed printings of sports agent Aaron Levy's roster of phenoms. Levy, who's followed JB since his days at Harvard Prep Academy, sits on the edge of his desk when he gives JB the news.

"The Olympic Committee made their decision. One spot goes to an eight-year league veteran, the second spot to a collegiate athlete."

JB leans back in a plush leather chair with clasped hands behind his head. "What's next?" he asks, seemingly unaffected by the news.

"My offer is for a million more, plus a signing bonus. The New Jersey team wants another year with the current salary."

"Call Chicago," JB tells him.

Levy pushes a button for the speaker. He has the number already on the speed dial. JB swivels to see a view of lower Manhattan. Outwardly, his Rolex, Eton oxford shirt, tailored slacks, and Ferragamo loafers give the impression of a man incapable of defeat. Right now, he's crushed. Deflated. He already hears sports analysts with ESPN and other news outlets give their opinions on why he's not winning.

There was an article written about him in a sports journal magazine with the title, "*The Normal Side of Losing*." In it, they highlight his success in high school and his early years at USC. Like always, there is mention of the situation involving Madeline. Controversial in that he was twenty and she just seventeen—the nature of their relations were considered statutory rape, which in certain instances was a felony in California. The article insinuates from that moment the game of basketball pivoted and went downhill for JB.

"This is it. The call that could change your career," Levy says to him.

"Free agency. It's like standing at the edge of a cliff," JB responds as he listens to the phone ring.

The manager of the Chicago team answers.

"Aaron Levy, phenom sports. I've got a free agent who could light up your court. JB's hungry for a championship."

"JB? As in the guy with the killer mid-range and fade-away jumpers?" the team manager asks.

JB leans in. "That's me. I'm ready to bring that fire to your team."

"JB, we need more than stats. We need heart. Why should we bet on you?"

"I've got heart. I've got hustle. And I've got a hunger for that ring. Plus, I'm a team player—no ego. Let's build something special."

"Alright, JB. We'll fly you in for a workout. But remember, we're chasing banners, not headlines."

"I'm ready to prove it. Let's write history together," JB tells him.

And so, in that pivotal phone call, JB's fate hung in the balance—a negotiation that could define his legacy.

Levy opens a sports magazine and flips to a page with JB sporting men's briefs. "Every woman wishes her man could look like this. They can't keep them in stock."

JB looks at the image of himself. He's shirtless wearing only a pair of white briefs. Some athletes get sneaker endorsements. Some athletes endorse soft drinks. JB graces glossies, daytime television commercials and gigantic billboards like the one hovering over Times Square. Since the campaign started earlier this year, his notoriety has escalated, and random people approach him asking the question: boxer or briefs? Now he opts for a chauffeured town car, except in the early mornings when he jogs in Central Park.

Anna Palermo, a friend who's a publicist dating back to his days at USC, is in town. A page with her code and a phone number scrolls across his pager. Before getting into the car, he finds the nearest pay phone booth.

"Hey. Perfect timing. Just left Levy's," he tells her.

"That son of a bitch," she replies.

"Damn. What's up?"

"How much time do you have, and how soon can you get over here?"

"I'm downtown. Sounds urgent."

"Opportunity knocks, and I immediately thought of you, Big Bad Wolf." She calls him the nickname given to him when he pledged undergrad at USC.

"Oh boy." A smile emanates from his lips. Simultaneously, a woman in a fitted skirt catches his eye as she struts with a bold and confident gait.

"I'm always finding ways of keeping you relevant," Anna adds.

"Got me curious," he says. His eyes follow the woman who's now lost in a crowd of countless pedestrians.

"Meet me inside the Oak Room at the Plaza," she tells him.

Anna prefers the old-school luxurious, posh accommodation of the Plaza Hotel. When JB arrives, she's seated at the bar. They greet each other with cheek-to-cheek kisses.

"If looking good were a crime, you would have been arrested several times," she says as soon as they sit. She notices monogrammed cufflinks and size fifteen, chestnut-colored Ferragamos. "Ever considered modeling for real?"

"Hell no." He frowns.

"You should. There are no guarantees—roll an ankle, tear an ACL, your career is over. Kaput."

"I didn't come all the way from downtown to hear this."

Anna chuckles. Her teeth, the whitest of white, are gleaming. Her nose is smaller, pert, and upturned. Her couture asymmetrical top caresses surgically enhanced 38 DDs. For such a petite frame, they are extremely excessive. Her father is a plastic surgeon with a thriving practice in Beverly Hills. Nose jobs and silicone breast implants come as birthday presents.

"My bags are packed for Barcelona." Anna is so excited, her brown eyes sparkle.

"I'm not going."

"What do you mean you're *not going*?" Just like that, her expression turns glum.

"Didn't make the cut."

"But you were an eminent prospect."

"I know."

"Damn." She reaches inside her small designer bag and retrieves a cigarette. First strike, a reason JB never fully got into a relationship with her. First time they met years ago at USC, when she was a senior and he a first-year student, they had sex, and when they finished, she lit a cigarette. He couldn't decide whether to pat himself on the back for having laid one of the sexiest co-eds on campus or be turned off by the stench of Virginia Slims on her breath.

"I'm calling that committee, and I'm protesting their decision," she tells him.

"No, you're not."

"Yes, I am."

"Anna, stop."

"Your numbers speak for themselves."

"And as phenomenal as they are, they just weren't enough."

They order lunch and a round of beer and spirits.

"What does Aaron say?" Anna asks.

"Nothing."

"Who did they select?" she asks.

"I don't remember," JB lies.

"I'm not watching. I will watch the track-and-field events, though. The rest can kiss my ass."

"They wouldn't mind," JB replies.

Anna catches his sideward glance and the flirty, enchanting way he smiles. The server arrives with their drinks.

"My homey," he says to her once the server leaves and they toast. He drinks from an ice-cold mug. "Now what's so damn important?"

"I've a client opening a nightspot, Uptown. He needs faces to drop in for an hour to make an appearance. He's shelling out twenty grand just to walk in, have a drink, mingle for a minute then leave. Now I wouldn't approach you with this if he wasn't A-list."

"Do I know him?"

"Who doesn't?" Anna proceeds to rap a couple of bars.

JB recognizes the lyrics and raps along with her. "Hell yeah. I'm down. When is it?"

"This Saturday."

"Same day as Maddie's graduation."

"Graduation ceremonies are usually done early, like way early. It'll be much later before you make an appearance."

"But it's a big day for Maddie."

"Just bring her."

"Think she'll be down?"

"Of course, with her gorgeous, lovely, fluffy self."

"Don't talk about my wife."

"Fluffy is good. I never knew that was your thing, too, but to each his own." She waves her highball glass before taking a sip.

Their food arrives, and in typical Hollywood fashion, Anna takes two forkfuls before she slides the plate away from her.

"Something wrong?" JB asks.

"No. I'm finished." She sips her vodka and Perrier. She's quiet and in deep thought. "Promise to keep a secret?" she says after seconds of silence.

JB, chewing, wipes each corner of his mouth. "I don't want to be privy to anything that'll come back and bite me."

"Trust me, I'm not mentioning this to another soul. My little sister, Mona, called me. She appeared in a couple of episodes of The Show. She regarded the star of The Show as a father figure, a mentor, someone to help guide her in the business. Well, she went out to dinner with him, and he ordered cocktails. She said she woke up naked in a hotel room, and it felt like she had been asleep for days."

"Where was he?"

"She doesn't remember all the details."

JB chews silently. "Sounds fishy."

"Like rape." Anna gets the server's attention, and he removes her plate of barely touched salad. "Your friend, Lilly, has she mentioned anything about him in that regard?" She retrieves the unlit cigarette from earlier.

"No. Just that he's a controlling asshole, and if he wanted, he could make or break you."

"I wish Mona had gone to the hospital and gotten examined."

"How long ago was this?" JB asks.

"She said it happened last year. She's just telling me this now. I feel like I need to report it, but he's so powerful, influential, and well connected. Who do you think they'll believe?"

"A guy like that, I'm sure he's done it to more than one. It's just a matter of them all coming together and taking him down. Every Goliath has his day with a hard rock."

"I'm not letting him get away with it." She finishes off her glass. "As much as I would love to spend time with you every day, some days I *actually* have stuff to do, but first I'll need a smoke. See you Saturday."

JB nods and finishes the rest of his lunch and beer alone at the bar.

****

Later that evening, from across the street, Basha watches JB and Madeline enter their apartment building. She waits minutes as she's done on and off for some time for the lights in their sixth-floor apartment to come on. Once, she tried taking the elevator up, but she didn't know the code on the keypad. The doorman wasn't always present, but one day he questioned her reason for a visit. She showed her credentials and informed him she was a well-known fashion photographer's assistant, scouting out a location for a possible fashion photo shoot. Once inside the building, she took the stairs and made the trek up to their floor, but nerves got the best of her.

Why can't I stop lurking and let go? He's not my man anymore. He's moved on with his life.

She didn't take JB seriously the day he told her their relationship was done. They'd broken up and reconciled several times before. In her mind, they were made for each other. They understood each other. They met during freshman orientation at USC, both Angelenos—he from Baldwin Hills, she from Leimert Park. She was tall and graceful like a swan, with a dancer's body, which caught his eye. They were both business majors and enrolled in the same classes. She always provided him with notes on the days he missed due to his demanding basketball schedule. She'd take naps during the day so she could break curfew and study with him after hours at his apartment on campus, typically between 12:30 and 4:30 in the morning. USC has always prided itself on having a powerhouse football team, and that excitement carried over to basketball season. JB, along with his close friends Caleb and Jake, was unstoppable on the court, with a running game punctuated with three-point hail Mary's and gravity-defying alley-oops. JB's monster dunks were so powerful the rim echoed in the arena.

Everyone on campus knew him, and when he and Basha walked together, everyone wanted to stop and chat. JB, being the big man on campus, happily engaged them. He never officially told her that she was his girl, never mentioned her whenever they asked him in interviews if there was someone special. She assumed the role—massaging his muscles with sports cream after a demanding home game, nursing bruises from a rough night of hazing when he pledged undergrad. She met his parents—mother was nice, the father, not so much. He even met her parents. His good looks and charm won them instantly. He was winning and scoring on and off campus.

She'd see him between classes walking with other girls and confront him.

"These are my fans," he'd tell her.

She wasn't a fool. She knew what was up. To get his attention, she maxed out a credit card and got new boobs. He noticed. Then it was back to seeing him when she could—spending nights at his apartment when he allowed her to and putting their relationship on a schedule until the day he told her they were done.

Her friend Rachael was a registered nurse working alongside a prominent obstetrician near Santa Monica. Rachael told Sasha about a new patient, a young girl about seventeen years old. Because she was still a minor, her father had to fill out her paperwork. The father was a world-renowned minister from Houston. On the first visit, the young girl was stressing that the father of the unborn child hadn't arrived from USC. Throughout the visits she and the young girl chatted, and Rachael put together pieces of the puzzle. When she finished, she couldn't wait to share it with Basha.

The lights are on at the apartment. Basha stands watching until she decides to leave. Walking to the subway, her mind races. The city with its countless aromas, wailing sirens, players shifting cards in games of three-card monte, even the talented street performers aren't enough to distract her from her thoughts.

Madeline's living the life I'm supposed to be living with the man I'm supposed to be with.

She came to New York from L.A. after spending three months in jail for burglarizing and vandalizing Madeline's property. She destroyed Madeline's piano, shredded nearly two hundred pages of original music, she even bleached and cut up Madeline's clothing. She wanted her to suffer like she was suffering.

She did hold on to one valuable item.

The subway headed for downtown is crowded, and now a group of youth turn on a boom box and dance. Others around pretend nothing is happening. Basha looks straight ahead, listening to subway brakes come to a screeching halt. She emerges from the subway and out to her neighborhood of Flatbush to her basement apartment. She turns on the light and looks over her file. She opens it, and there are photos. Photos of Madeline having lunch with Lynnwood, photos of JB walking in Central Park with Lilly, and photos of Madeline entering a building believed to be an abortion clinic. She waited nearly two hours to capture a photo of Madeline leaving the clinic and being helped to a waiting cab. She opens a trunk where she keeps her valuables and pulls out a pearl necklace. It belongs to Madeline, and Basha imagines it must've cost a pretty penny.

She sits in her apartment. She should go back to California and complete those twenty credits toward her bachelor's degree in business, mind her own business and use her eye for photography to capture celebrity life or better yet, get her own life. But she is so close. So close to making life miserable for JB the way he has made life miserable for her.

Eight

Madeline awakens with JB still asleep. His cheek rests atop the pillowy softness of her right breast. She sees Melody sleeping peacefully in the crook of her left arm. The blissful tenderness of the moment brings her to the realization she is the most fortunate girl in the world. The ceiling fan whirls quietly, and although there is a slight chill in the air, she's nestled between JB and Melody where it's warm and cozy. She kisses JB on the forehead and runs aimless fingers through his curls. The movement stirs him awake. His eyes adjust, and shortly afterward, his mouth lands on the lusciousness of Madeline's lips.

"Somebody's graduating from Juilliard today," he whispers.

"Pinch me. Really pinch me," she tells him.

"I have something else in mind." He smiles and kisses her lips. They've long gotten past the morning breath phase.

"I'll make a conscious effort to be in the moment, and not get too excited," she says.

"Do whatever you feel. You've earned it."

Melody stirs and stretches, making cute little stretching sounds. She opens her eyes and notices her parents.

"Look who's awake." Madeline brings her closer for a kiss on the cheek.

Melody wipes her eyes and cuddles closer to Madeline. The joy of still being loved and needed, despite days of separation, inspired Madeline to write a symphony. Melody has her own room, but when she comes to the city, she wants to snuggle under the comfort and protection of her mother.

The phone rings constantly as calls of well wishes are pouring in from family, former colleagues, and close-knit members of her father's church who have known Madeline since childhood. A call-waiting signal alerts her of another call. She glances at the clock to see she has two hours before the commencement ceremony and she still needs to get Melody dressed.

"Hello," she answers.

"Madeline, it's Lynnwood."

"Hi."

"Sending my regrets. Sorry I can't be there to see you walk across that stage," he says.

"It's all good. I'm glad you called."

"Next time I see you, you will be a Juilliard grad. From this day forward, I'm holding you to a higher standard."

"I appreciate the challenge, and I'll strive to meet those expectations," Madeline says just as JB walks up from behind and gives her a kiss on the neck.

"You're not taking any more phone calls after this. We've got to get going," JB whispers.

Madeline hears him, but she's also listening to Lynnwood. "You've got the chops—the technique, the heart. Europe's waiting for us." He tells her. She says her good-byes and hangs up, staring at the phone. She imagines the adventure that lay ahead.

"Who was that?" JB asks while lathering his face with shaving cream.

"Lynnwood Tremé," she answers.

"He's a trumpet player, right?" JB looks at her reflection staring back at him from the bathroom mirror. "I don't recall meeting him."

"I was hoping you got the opportunity today, but he's not coming."

"Was he a professor, too?"

"More like a mentor. He's invited me on the tour."

Looking in the mirror, JB applies an electric shaver to his face. "The tour where you want to take our daughter and stay gone for five months?"

"Now that you're not going to Barcelona, you can join us."

The reality of Madeline's statement strikes a sensitive nerve. Not being chosen this time for the Olympic team reminds him of losing. The fact of Madeline leaving and possibly taking Melody with her feels like losing. As he stands there, towel slung over his shoulder, the bathroom walls seem to close in on him. The mirror reflects more than his physical form; it reveals insecurity. As time draws closer to Madeline stepping into her graduation gown, he wonders if he is enough. Can he compete with European stages, with standing ovations? Madeline deserves to chase her music, to play her piano in ancient halls. But deep down, he wonders if their love can continue to thrive.

Hours later, Madeline steps off the stage, her heart still racing from the applause that reverberated through the grand auditorium. The weight of her degree in her hand feels like a promise—a culmination of years of dedication, late-night rehearsals, and the unwavering belief that music can bridge worlds.

Be in the moment. Remember its extraordinary significance, despite being a young mother and a wife, balancing those roles while holding steady on a tightrope—you are now a Juilliard graduate. She reads her degree: The Juilliard School, be it known that Madeline May Richardson has completed the studies and satisfied the requirements for the degree of Bachelor of Music.

She embraces her father and Gilda. It's emotional, for each re-members years and hours of work dedicated to getting to this moment.

Outside the school, hundreds of graduates with their families and friends mill about the area. The atmosphere is festive. It's a pleasant spring Saturday in New York City, and the lighting is perfect for pictures. James and Judy gather along with Madeline's Aunt Mary and her cousins Cassandra, Caleb, and Rosie. Frenchy snaps a family photo. In it, he captures as many as he can who came to celebrate Madeline and can fit within the camera's range of focus. Soon, Gilda herds everyone into a super stretch limo she's chartered for the occasion. It takes scenic routes through Manhattan. There's a moment during the ride, Kool and the Gang's "Celebration" plays from the speakers, and everyone sings on cue with the chorus, especially the part of the song when they yell, "Yahoo."

Twenty minutes later, the limo arrives at the entrance of the North building of the World Trade Center. Madeline holds JB's hand inside the expansive lobby while he carries Melody with his right arm. They walk to a set of elevators, and once inside, JB presses the button for the 106th floor. The door opens to more guests who yell, "Congratulations." Madeline recognizes familiar faces from her father's church. She's moved to tears while she embraces them and receives their well wishes. The Windows on the World restaurant boasts spectacular views of the Manhattan skyline. This isn't her first visit; she and JB had a romantic dinner here last year for her twenty-first birthday. JB always seems to impress her without even trying—impromptu horse and carriage rides in the city, VIP helicopter tours of Manhattan. Now this. A lifelike drawing of her inside a gilded picture frame sitting before a grand piano is prominent near the entrance. Madeline examines it.

"Thank you, Rosie," she cries.

Rosie, the artist, is now nineteen. She was fourteen when Madeline first saw her sketching away in her sketchpad. She was a regular attendee when Aunt Mary operated a youth center. They met when Madeline volunteered one summer. There was something remarkable and special about Rosie. Aunt Mary noticed it, too, and later adopted her. She and Madeline embrace.

"I love it," Madeline tells her.

"That means everything, I'm glad you love it," Rosie says.

Madeline's cousin Cassandra wraps her arms around Madeline and squeezes her with a hug. "You've definitely inspired me."

"How?"

"So many times, I've wanted to quit flying airplanes. The pressure of having something to prove because I'm a woman and because I'm Black—I don't want to give them the benefit of thinking I can't handle it."

"Maybe one day we'll sit down and exchange horror stories," Madeline tells her.

"I have so many I can write a book," Cassandra replies.

"Me too," Rosie adds.

Gilda and Eugene stand before family and close friends once they are all seated. A photographer inconspicuously walks the room capturing candid shots. "My wife, Gilda, and I take this opportunity to thank each of you in this room. This occasion is an answered prayer—a dream fulfilled. Each one of you contributed to this moment, whether you helped with raising and nurturing Madeline's daughter, Melody." He acknowledges James and Judy with a nod. "Attending her recitals, sending her care packages, calling to offer words of encouragement... You are here because you all played a part, and for that, we are grateful."

Eugene and Gilda approach the table where Madeline sits. JB is next to her holding her hand.

"Gilda and I are proud of you. I am reminded of Galatians the sixth chapter and ninth verse where it reads, 'And let us not grow weary of doing good, for in due season we will reap, if we do not give up,' You've inspired me."

"And me," Gilda adds. "There's no limit to what you can't do. No matter how taxing or impossible the task, your tenacious spirit is determined to see it through."

Madeline's eyes brim with tears as she remembers long days and nights spent working and studying—at one point, managing on just four hours of sleep. The wait staff brings out silver trays and gives out flutes of sparkling cider. Eugene and Gilda lift their glasses as Madeline, JB, and about twenty-five other guests do the same.

"Toast to you, Madeline. As you step into the next movement of your life, remember this: you are more than a pianist; you are a conductor of souls. Your crescendo awaits—may it be as breathtaking as the first note you ever played," Eugene says before taking a sip.

The room responds as tears of happiness stream down Madeline's cheeks. JB brings her in closer for a hug and a kiss.

"You did it," he tells her.

"Thank you," she mouths. She thinks of JB being on a team that struggles and him not getting selected to represent the U.S. this time around in the Olympics, how he dropped out of college and went pro so he could provide for her and Melody. Now she's the one with a college degree about to embark on her dreams of traveling Europe with a renowned musician with a respected orchestra. Part of her feels guilty.

She stands with flute in hand and salutes her guests. More wait staff enter with plates of arugula salads, followed by entree choices of chicken cordon blue or beef medallion. The celebration continues through the evening. As the sun sets, the chandeliers dim in the dining room creating a relaxing and intimate setting. A pianist plays "(They Long to Be) Close to You" by the Carpenters. Some of the guests pose for pictures. Frenchy, Caleb, James, and others sit laughing, drinking, and joking at the bar. Away from the guests, nestled in a secluded bay window alcove, Madeline sits comfortably on JB's lap. The evening sky is enchanting.

"First time we came here; I looked out and saw the Statue of Liberty. She looked like a Monopoly piece," Madeline tells him.

"Is that all you remember?" he asks.

Madeline studies him, reading his handsome features.

"It was my twenty-first birthday, and you ordered champagne," she tells him.

"Miss Tipsy After One Glass," he notes.

"Not something I'd try again."

JB takes a curly strand of Madeline's hair to place behind her ear. Her amethyst-and-diamond earrings sparkle. "I see you're wearing the earrings I gave you for your birthday."

"That was a wild, crazy night," she tells him.

"I remember," he replies. His expression is dreamy.

By now, most of the guests are leaving. Judy and James take Melody with them back to Madeline and JB's home in New Jersey. Her father and Gilda, along with Aunt Mary and Uncle Frenchy, come say their goodbyes. Madeline's cousins Cassandra, Caleb and Rosie talk of going to a taping of Def Comedy Jam. Melody and JB agree to connect with them afterward.

A brief time later, JB receives a page from Anna. She's arranged a stretch limo, bound for an appearance Uptown to pick them up. Once inside, JB loosens his tie and finds the button that closes the partition. Madeline opens the moonroof, and the sounds of the city emanate like music over a loudspeaker. Inside the limo, R &

B band, Mint Condition's "Forever in Your Eyes" plays. City winds blow the curls across her face. She raises her hands, and a surge of exhilaration comes over her. *If I can make it here, I can make it anywhere.*

"You should see it out here," she tells him.

"I like this view much better." She hears him, next she feels him take her right leg and place it over his left shoulder. She uses the opening of the moon roof to balance herself, feeling his hands cup her bottom and situating her body in a position so that his mouth stimulates the most intimate part of her. She looks down and notices movement underneath her dress.

Saturday night in the city—throngs of tourists are on the sidewalks and crosswalks. The stretch limo comes to an intersection to wait as several pedestrians cross. Madeline, in a fit of ecstasy, screams out from the moonroof.

A pack of pedestrians yells back, "Whooo hooo! Me too! I love New York!"

JB's large, strong hands tease and caress. Madeline grips them, holding on for dear life, while the euphoric sensation passes over her. He guides her back in, holding on to her. Her body is limp. He kisses and looks into her eyes, noticing a satisfied smile emerging from her lips.

There are streets in Manhattan where the traffic is gridlocked. A gentle breeze from the moon roof cools down the space, but the heat and passion between them continues. When the limo lurches to a complete stop, they adjust and fix themselves. JB grabs peppermints nearby, runs a hand through his curly high-top fade and removes his necktie. Madeline opens her pochette to apply a coat of lipstick. She notices searchlights and a large crowd of revelers. JB and Madeline emerge from the limo. The blinding flash of cameras and boisterous partygoers call out JB's name. Club bouncers remove velvet ropes and rush them into the night club. Holding on to JB's hand, Madeline's eyes adjust to the indigo haze, and the crowd inside. Music blasts, guests are plentiful. They both notice Anna approaching, dressed in a white Valentino laser-cut, short-sleeved mini dress, showcasing her curved, shapely legs.

"My favorite people." She greets both with cheek-to-cheek air kisses.

A rap group performs onstage. The lead rapper stops mid-performance.

"JB is in the motherfucking building. Show some love," he dictates in a rough Jamaican-accented growl.

The crowd cheers, and the noise in the packed club is deafening. Madeline notices women dressed in next to nothing emerge from all corners of the room. Anna ushers JB and Madeline to a VIP section complete with magnums of champagne chilled over ice.

"Congratulations, graduate," Anna leans in to say once they are seated.

"Thank you," Madeline replies.

JB recognizes two players from the league. He leaves Madeline and Anna to greet and converse with them.

"I love your style," Anna continues to yell over the music, admiring Madeline's mauve-flared cocktail dress.

"Thanks," Madeline replies. Her cordial dealing with Anna only happens when JB is around. Before Madeline became deeply involved with JB, she was told by her cousin Cassandra that JB and Anna once had relations. Although JB admitted he only slept with her twice, Madeline's intuition senses differently.

JB rejoins them, placing himself in the middle. Madeline notices Anna cross her legs inward toward JB, brushing the side of her Manolo Blahnik pumps against his trouser leg. The gesture is so comfortable and automatic for her, she doesn't notice Madeline's reaction.

"It's only an hour," Anna yells at him. "Can you handle it?"

JB leans near her ear. "Think he'll drop extra if we want to stay longer?" He looks at her and winks. He notices Madeline quietly observing, her upper lip curled in a slight air of disdain.

"You good?" It's something she notices he asks often when they're out at large gatherings like this and she's quiet. Before she answers, someone else catches his attention, and he stands to greet him. Soon Anna joins them, and the three converse before she steps aside and allows them to pose for a picture.

Having accompanied JB to promotional events in the past, Madeline's come to expect the atmosphere, much like a basketball game, loud with a cast of characters with colorful personalities. JB introduces her to the rap mogul and owner of the club who kisses her hand.

"Those eyes," he tells her.

JB takes her other hand. "That's what got me in trouble. Couldn't stop staring into them."

They pose for a picture. "Real party is upstairs," he tells JB.

"I'm game." JB looks at Madeline.

"Lead the way," she tells the rap mogul.

An elevator ride up several floors and up a flight of stairs, JB and Madeline emerge on the rooftop among a more exclusive crowd of partiers. Madeline spots several celebrities from the New York performance scene. The atmosphere isn't as loud, despite being several flights up from the bustling streets of Harlem. The rap mogul introduces JB and Madeline to the crème de la crème of celebrities. Among them is an internationally critically acclaimed singer with multiple awards under her belt. The songbird greets and chats with JB and Madeline as if she's known them for years.

"I heard about you," she says to JB. Madeline notices beads of perspiration settling on her brow and top lip.

"Believe none of what you hear and half of what you see," JB tells her.

The songbird has a tic where she sniffs and rubs her nose. "Oh, I can believe this," she says. "I'm sure your wife will confirm it."

Madeline is listening carefully.

"I was told that you are the bomb when it comes to writing a love song," she declares.

JB is shocked. "Who told you that?"

"Don't worry about who," she says.

Madeline notices the songbird's speaking voice is raspy, but when she sings, her powerhouse vocals soar like an eagle.

"I think I know who you're talking about," JB says to her.

The songbird notes his reaction. "You know you're the shit."

"I am. That's why they call me Dr. Funkenstein," he tells her.

"Why?" she asks.

"I'm in the studio creating monster hits."

"Get out of here, boy." Her laugh sounds more like a smoker's cackle. She wipes her nose.

JB is flattered she gets his humor.

The songbird, who's probably 115 pounds soaking wet, takes his hand. "Let's get started. I don't believe in putting off tomorrow what I can do right now."

JB notices the songbird is under the influence of something. He blows it off, seeing that in an instant she totally forgot about their conversation and starts another with someone else.

They were only supposed to stay for an hour and connect with Caleb, Cassandra and Rosie but ended up partying into the wee hours of the morning. It's a little after four a.m. when JB and

Madeline arrive at their apartment. They notice a manila envelope addressed to them waiting at the door.

"Why didn't he just leave this in the mailbox?" JB scoffs, referring to their mail carrier.

Madeline reads the words written in bold letters: **Photos. Do Not Bend.**

"I wasn't expecting photos. Were you?" she asks.

"No." He opens the door and flicks on the lights to their apartment.

They find a spot on the couch, and JB uses a letter opener for the envelope. Inside is a small stack of eight-by-ten photos. The first photo shows him and Lilly in an embrace. She appears distraught holding on to him.

"What the hell?" Madeline asks. "Explain this."

Nine

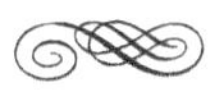

JB can't believe his eyes as he flips to the next photo. It captures Lilly in front, and he is just a couple of paces behind, ascending steps to her apartment building. The next photo shows him opening the door, allowing her to enter. Another photo captures them sitting close together on a park bench, presumably in Central Park, both of their eyes concealed behind dark shades. The following photo shows him kissing her forehead. The next photo shows them captured at a different time. Her head rests on his shoulder, her arm is clasped around his, and their hands are intertwined.

"Explain this. What's happening?"

"Believe me, it's not what it looks like."

"Then what is it? First, I walk in on you talking to her on the phone with your hand in your boxers, like you're having phone sex. Now these. What's happening here?" She picks up the photo of them on the bench and him kissing Lilly's forehead.

"I told you before, Lilly and Benny are going through a rough patch. She reached out to me because she knew Benny and I had been working in the studio. Initially, she was picking my brain for information, trying to see if I would tell her some things."

"You're kissing her. Look at it." She brings the photo up to his face.

"Believe me, nothing happened. When Lilly invited me into her apartment, she poured her heart out to me about her and Benny's marriage. The entire time I was there, not once did I get the urge to want to sleep with her."

"I don't believe you." The anger building up inside of Madeline has her trembling.

"What you see is me being a friend—I'm listening, I'm comforting and offering my shoulder to cry on."

"She used to be your girl, JB. Don't lie to me."

"Maddie, I promise we didn't do anything."

"It looks like you were meeting her on the regular."

"We did, but trust me, nothing happened. She's overly affectionate. She respects that I have a wife and a family. At that moment, she wanted someone she could vent her frustration to. They have a daughter around Melody's age. The Show just ended so she's out of work, Benny is screwing around, and I just happened to be there to talk her off the ledge."

"Have you been sleeping with Anna again?" Madeline asks.

"Are you serious, Maddie?" JB looks appalled by the question.

"You can't tell me all the times you've worked with her that you don't get the urge."

"I'm not answering that." He chuckles.

"Because it's true."

"You sound crazy right now."

"I saw how she brushed up against you tonight. I saw you looking at the women parading in front of you at the club. I'm sure they were hoping for the opportunity to catch you alone, away from me."

"Now you're letting your imagination get the best of you."

"I'm not imagining anything. I have proof." She looks at the photos. There are more.

The next photo shows Madeline sitting across from Lynnwood at a restaurant. Another photo shows them getting caught in the rain as they make a dash for a waiting cab. A different photo zooms in on the words, *Excellence in Reproductive Healthcare Clinic.* The following photo shows a female staffer with the clinic pushing Madeline in a wheelchair. Madeline looks weary, and her curly hair is disheveled.

"Where did these come from?" Madeline asks, searching the envelope. All she sees is her and JB's names typed on an address label with no sender's information. JB examines the photo closely, his eyes flit as he tries to make sense of it.

"What the fuck is this?" He shows her the photos of her being wheeled out of the building.

Every nerve in Madeline's body throbs and pulsates. The photo recalls the dreaded discovery. The procedure. The sterile environment. The days following, lying around her apartment with the curtains drawn in darkness. Her course load and performance schedule at Juilliard were taxing. Another child she didn't need.

"I...ummm...I wasn't ready." She scours her brain searching for the right words—to soften the blow.

"Ready for what?" JB anticipates her answer.

"Another pregnancy." Her throat catches.

"What?" JB studies her expression, searching for an explanation.

With eyes filled with pain and sorrow, she looks directly at him. "I wasn't ready."

JB looks at the photo. "Please tell me that's not what I think it is."

Madeline's ears ring, their intensity sounding like a series of fire alarms setting off.

"Please tell me you didn't do what I think you did." The tone of JB's voice teeters somewhere between calm and on the verge of erupting.

"I was going to tell you."

Madeline has no words, just a stinging, ringing sensation in her ears, and every hair on her body stands at attention. JB closes his eyes and lowers his head. "Tell me you didn't do what you did," he repeats.

Without a word, she lowers her head as the tears pour.

"Who's baby?" JB comes closer.

The question catches Melody off guard. "What do you mean?"

"Don't play with me, Maddie."

"What are you asking?"

"Are you fucking that trumpet player?"

His tone startles her. "You think Lynnwood and I are lovers?" she asks.

"You tell me."

The photos and the sharp tone of their conversation has Madeline's head spinning.

"Just like you're having a hard time believing me, never in a million years did I think I'd be thinking the same about you," he says to her.

The intensity of JB's words cut like a thousand tiny slices.

"Whose baby?" he asks again.

"I can't believe you're asking me this. It was yours," she declares.

"I thought you were on the pill."

"I am."

"You must've missed a bunch of days."

She wipes the tears falling from her eyes. JB shakes his head as the realization of Maddie's action sinks in. "When did you have the procedure?" he asks.

"Last spring."

"You remember the date?"

"Sometime in April."

"How far along were you?"

"Nine weeks."

"Why didn't you tell me?"

Madeline shakes her head.

"You killed our baby."

Madeline closes her eyes, feeling more tears roll down the sides of her face. "We didn't need another child."

"You made that decision alone. You never once considered how I felt."

"We don't spend enough quality time with Melody. What were we going to do with another child—let your mother raise it, too? I'm sorry, I'm sorry."

"Sorry? Just sorry? Are you freaking kidding me?" His tone and words continue to slice and slash. He stands and walks inside their bedroom, slamming the door behind him. Madeline looks at the photos as a mixture of anger, sadness and anxiety consumes her. Who is behind these photos? How long had they been following them? How did they get inside the building?

* * *

He wishes she hadn't fallen asleep next to him. She's wearing a silk nightgown, which is rare around him. At bedtime, he preferred her naked, so when the urge to make love to her hit him, there was no hindrance. Their endless rounds of lovemaking had no limits nor boundaries. Eighty-two games, half of them away, made coming home and making love to her that much sweeter. Her kisses were always passionate, gentle, and attentive. After seeing the photos of her with Lynnwood, he's questioning that sweet, innocent girl. *It's the quiet ones you least expect.* It wouldn't be the first time she'd gone behind another guy's back. When they met, she was with someone else. JB met him once; on the same day it was discovered Madeline was pregnant. She delivered a knockout punch to the boyfriend—told him she was pregnant, and the baby wasn't his. She is gifted, cultured and attractive with a body not lacking in areas considered the most desirable. Her breasts are more than a mouthful. Other parts of her body, he delights in. He could easily understand just how a man like Lynnwood would want to collaborate musically with her. He did, and the music they created was magical and sweet to the ears. One hit of Madeline gave him a high that left him hooked.

"Wake up." The resonance of his voice shakes the room.

"I am up," she says. Her back faces him. He sees the crisscross straps of her silk gown.

"Look at me," he tells her.

She turns to face him. Her eyes are swollen from having cried herself to sleep.

"What's happening to us?" he asks.

Again, his words pierce and slice.

"We're drifting apart," she answers.

His handsome Black and Filipino features are vivid and expressive. "Remember the night when I asked your Pops for your hand in marriage, and he talked to us about love? He even gave us a biblical verse. I still remember what it says." JB quotes it, "Love is patient, love is kind and not jealous; love does not brag and is not arrogant. It is not proud. It does not dishonor others, it is not self-seeking, it is not easily angered, it keeps no record of wrongs. Love does not delight in evil but rejoices with the truth. Love always protects, always trusts, always hopes, always perseveres. Love never fails. I read this to remind myself why I committed to us."

Madeline feels a tear roll down her cheek. "I know I haven't always put my love into action. I realized it was wrong, but I couldn't handle another responsibility. Daddy made me go through the first pregnancy. I never wanted this or for you to be in this situation."

"Stop. I didn't marry you because you were pregnant, and I didn't marry you to stay out of jail. I did it because I love you. I love being a father. I love our little girl. It's hard for me to accept what you did, especially now that I can take care of you. We can grow our family. I want a tribe with you, Maddie."

A soft sob escapes Madeline. Feelings of guilt. Now that Melody is a tangible, whole beautiful human being, there are still times Madeline wishes she could've ended it. Her intentions have always been to finish Juilliard and travel the world performing classical music. She didn't want children; she didn't want a husband. Her marriage to JB was her father's way of easing his conscience and maintaining his decency and standards—her Aunt Mary called it, "Shotgun marriages do not last."

Madeline was seven months pregnant when she walked down the aisle. Her sheltered life never prepared her for the emotional gymnastics she would face.

JB sighs. "Are you seeing him?"

"Lynnwood? No! Absolutely not. Our relationship is professional. Lynnwood has always been professional. Those photos were taken of us out having lunch discussions about the tour. He's never flirted with me. He's never talked inappropriately to me. He's always remained professional. I wouldn't be going on tour with him if he weren't."

JB is quiet. *Dude is either a Poindexter or gay.* He can't understand how a man can be around a woman as fine as Madeline and remain professional. He had to check a couple of teammates in the locker room for remarks they made referring to Madeline as Jessica Rabbit, the voluptuous cartoon character from the movie, *Who Framed Roger Rabbit?*

At times, marriage to JB can be mentally frustrating. Madeline wants to trust him. By the same token, she doesn't want to be a fool. She can't shake the photo of him kissing Lilly's forehead.

"You can't tell me you don't have deeper feelings for Lilly," she cries.

"I don't. I promise you. I told you my relationship with her was brief, and during that time, I didn't care about being in a high-profile relationship. We both realized we were better off as friends."

"What about Anna?"

"What about her?" he asks.

"She's touchy-feely with you—and that's around me—so, I can only imagine when it's just you two."

"She's a people person."

"That doesn't make it right," Madeline replies.

"Look, we keep it professional. Anna looks out for me; she makes moves on my behalf so we can maintain this lifestyle long after I stop balling."

"I thought that was Levy's sole purpose."

"He handles my business. Anna connects me with the culture. Now, you don't need to worry about Lilly, Anna, or any other chick that I've been with."

"Who do you think took the photos?" Madeline asks.

"My guess is these crazy, money hungry photographers who sell celebrity photos to gossip magazines," JB responds.

"If that was the case, why would they leave them with us?" Madeline asks.

"Beats me." He sighs.

"I don't feel safe in this building. Whoever took those photos bypassed the door attendant. They're stopping at nothing to destroy us. We need to talk to him first thing Monday morning," Madeline declares.

Now with Madeline graduated, JB doesn't see the need to keep the apartment. Hopefully, from their meeting with the door attendant, they'd discover who left the package and how soon they could move out.

Ten

"Musical Odyssey: A Classical Landscape" is in the press release for the European tour. Lynnwood and Madeline do press junkets from different media outlets like The New York Times, Public Broadcasting Stations, and National Public Radio. Lynnwood and Madeline visit a public school in Harlem where they perform in front of fourth and fifth graders. Madeline plays the first movement of Mozart's "Piano Sonata k545." She and Lynnwood and a trio of violinists then play the third movement of Antonio Vivaldi's "Summer."

"For some children, their only taste of the arts is when we bring it to them," Lynnwood says.

A promotional tour poster shows Lynnwood. He's prominent and dressed in a black tuxedo holding a shiny brass trumpet featuring guests Madeline M. Richardson with the Tremé orchestra. The first city on the European tour is London.

Between press junkets and promotion, Madeline searches for potential candidates to be Melody's nanny. She believes she's found someone. The wife of one of JB's teammates referred a potential candidate from an agency with glowing reviews. After a background check to prove she has no red flags, Madeline sets up a nanny trial day with Melody. The girl, who's nineteen, is bright and energetic and has a good rapport with Melody. After she leaves, Judy pulls Madeline aside.

"Don't hire her. She's too attractive, and you don't want her near your husband."

"Then what do I do?" A look of desperation crosses Madeline's face.

"James and I will continue to care for her, and we will fly out to see you between touring when you get breaks. You *will* get breaks, right?" Judy asks.

"Yes."

"Are you done nanny searching?" Judy asks.

Madeline sighs, "I guess I am. Look, I can't thank you and James enough." Tears blur Madeline's eyes.

Judy notices. "Why the tears?"

"All my life, I've dreamed of this opportunity. Never did I imagine having JB and Melody to consider. I've missed many milestones in Melody's life. I only want her with me because I don't want to continue missing out. I know what it's like to long for a mother's warm embrace, even when she's no longer there."

"There are times when she asks about you, but I always tell her how much you love her. It isn't always easy, but sometimes you make sacrifices to be great."

Madeline remembers Gilda's words to her, words that her deceased mother once shared: Madeline has an anointing upon her. Her music will touch souls across oceans. *But what about the little four-year-old soul she cradles in her arms? The one who calls her Mommy.*

Madeline has mixed feelings when the day arrives for her to leave.

"I don't want you to go," JB tells her. He watches her pack articles of clothing inside a Louis Vuitton steamer trunk.

"Stop." She waves him off while continuing to pack.

"Whatever they're paying, I'll double it."

He follows her inside their custom bedroom closet. She grabs a pair of black Jimmy Choo kitten heels and a pair of red Stuart Weitzman pointed toe stilettos.

"You don't need those. Remember, you only wear them for me."

"I'll have them on hand in case you decide you want to get freaky in Helsinki."

"Apparently you didn't hear me."

"I heard you, JB."

"I need you."

"Stop. You're just making me feel guilty."

Madeline isn't trying to get distracted with him standing there shirtless and toned with hands in his pockets. The top of those famous briefs for which he's a spokesperson are peeking out from his joggers. She finds a team jersey that he had given her, brings it up to her nose and inhales.

"Still has your scent," she says before folding and placing it inside her luggage. "You never finished telling me about your trip to Chicago."

"I don't want to talk about that right now," he says, grabbing her hand and pulling her toward him.

"My flight leaves in three hours, and I still haven't showered."

"It's not too late for you to change your mind and stay."

"You're tripping." She moves out of his grasp.

"Five months is a long time. Did you and Gilda ever consider us when you booked this tour?"

"JB, you didn't marry a frivolous girl who wastes time, spends your money and hangs out gossiping with fake friends." She remembers what Judy told her when Madeline first started seeing JB, about having something to occupy her time. "I've got a career that needs to blossom. Not once since you've been in the NBA have I interfered with you. Now I need you to show the same respect for me."

He stands silent for a minute before he quietly walks out of their bedroom. An hour or so later, a driver pulls into the driveway of their New Jersey estate. Judy and Melody are nearby.

"Call Gilda if you need to contact me. I'll make sure to call and check on Melody."

Madeline hugs Melody, and suddenly it hits her, she's leaving her again. She kneels beside Melody. "Mommy's going to play music for a little while, but guess what? You, Daddy, Lola, and Lolo can fly out to see me, okay?"

Melody's eyes search Madeline's seeking assurance. "Will you miss me?" Melody asks.

Madeline feels tears. She kisses Melody's forehead and whispers, "Always."

Madeline notices JB approaching, thinking he's about to kiss and hug her goodbye. Instead, he takes Melody and plays with her. Melody giggles and laughs as he walks with her back inside the house. Madeline stands waiting.

Judy notices. "Listen, I'll deal with him." She gives Madeline a warm hug. Judy smiles, her eyes are misty. "I'm proud of you, doing your own thing."

Madeline nods as more tears flow. The driver loads her luggage into the vehicle, all the while she anticipates JB walking out the door and giving her a big sendoff, but he doesn't. No one is there to wave goodbye when the car pulls away.

* * *

Gilda notices Madeline staring out the airplane window for quite some time.

"Earth to Madeline." Gilda's voice is soothing.

Madeline continues to stare out the window. Gilda touches her shoulder. The gesture startles Madeline.

"You want to talk about it?" Gilda asks.

Madeline nods as her eyes become blurred with tears.

Gilda is attentive as they sit in the plush comfort of Business First seats aboard a Continental Airlines DC 10-30. A flight attendant informs them the flight would take approximately seven hours.

"JB didn't want me to leave. He wouldn't kiss me goodbye or anything. He was saying things like, 'Whatever they're paying you, I'll double it.' He knows better. I wasn't canceling this tour. I get it, he wants me to stay, but I've dreamed of this opportunity, and it's finally happening, and he's not happy for me."

"When we booked this, we took into consideration the timing of the tour would happen during his off-season. You told me you discussed it with JB, and everything was fine because he would be participating in the Olympic games in Barcelona." She recalls their conversation, which seemed like ages ago. "And as we know, that didn't happen." Madeline closes her eyes as tears start to flow. "This is supposed to be a happy moment."

Gilda opens her pocketbook to retrieve a handkerchief. Madeline takes it and wipes her eyes.

"At the first opportunity, give him a call and clear the air between you. The last thing you want is emotional distance. It's difficult enough being apart. You want peace and passion to prevail."

Madeline reflects upon the days since JB discovered the abortion and the photos of him with Lilly. To keep busy, she immersed herself with rehearsals while JB and his agent, Aaron Levy, jetted off to Chicago to watch the Chicago and Portland NBA teams in the playoffs.

Somewhere between rehearsals and meetings, they took an impromptu trip to a Jamaican retreat with Melody in tow. There they made sandcastles, snorkeled, got acquainted with the locals and traveled the countryside by jeep. At night after reading Melody bedtime stories and putting her to sleep, they retreated to the openness of their bedroom suite. The breeze off the Caribbean rustled the tiny hairs on Madeline's naked body, giving her goosebumps. Lovemaking sessions lasted to the point of exhaustion, and morning found her lying upon his chest, skin to skin, gazing upon his sleeping face, lovingly and tenderly stroking his curls. She wrestles with vulnerability and fragility.

Knowing JB could be lying about Lilly, Anna, or any other situation where infidelity came into question, there she was adoring and making love to him. Available on a whim to satisfy his urges while riding in the limo to the club uptown or home in the studio while creating music. When an impulse comes over JB, she goes from playing the baby grand to spread eagle on top of it, or leaned over the kitchen sink, or sprawled on the billiards table. She is tossed about, on her knees, in the pool, on the beach, on a boat sailing on the ocean. They are in an afternoon rain shower in the Costa Rican rainforest or tasting snowdrops, like they did on their honeymoon in the Sierra Mountains in Nevada. The urge comes, and it rushes in like a tidal wave.

"Am I being selfish?" Madeline asks.

"No, but you are ambitious."

"That's not a bad thing, is it?"

"No. The key is knowing how to balance it because as we know, when you focus on any one thing, everything around it becomes blurry out of focus."

Madeline opens her leather backpack where she keeps her original compositions and blank staff sheets. She retrieves a manila envelope, and inside are the photos of JB with Lilly. She told JB a lie, that the photos got lost when they were moving out of their New York apartment. She finds the photo of JB kissing Lilly's forehead and gives it to Gilda who frowns. Gilda finds a pair of glasses and puts them on to get a better look.

"What's the story behind this?" she asks, taking off her glasses and looking at Madeline.

"JB tells me they're only friends. She's having marital issues. Sounds like she might have financial issues—she's an actress, and the sitcom just ended its run. She's been crying on his shoulder. Literally."

Gilda puts on her glasses again. Madeline gives her the other photo of JB with Lilly embracing publicly. Lilly appears distraught, inconsolable, like she's holding on to him for dear life.

"He told you they were just friends. Have you met her?" Gilda asks.

"Years ago, when I spent the summer in L.A., JB introduced us, and I also met the guy who would eventually become her husband. He's a rock musician."

"I see." Gilda's eyes dance between the photos.

"What do you think?" Madeline asks.

Gilda removes her glasses. "I wouldn't be surprised if there is something."

"What do I do, Gilda?"

"Have that hard conversation. Is your marriage worth fighting for? Can you balance your career and marriage effectively? Are you willing to put your career aside and focus on motherhood and your marriage?" Gilda puts on her glasses.

"This will sound selfish, but I'm focusing on what makes me happy."

"And what is that?"

"The music." A fresh tear rolls down Madeline's cheek.

***

As soon as Madeline enters her hotel suite, she dials the international code for the U.S. followed by her home number. The phone picks up after the second ring. It's Judy.

"We've arrived," Madeline tells her.

"Great. How was the flight?"

"Not bad. Where's JB and Melody?"

"The three of us are on our way to the city to see Jelly's Last Jam."

"I've seen it. You'll love it."

"I finally used the new Polaroid you got me and snapped several pictures of Melody with her ponytails and ruffles. You should see her poses. She's not camera shy."

"I'll just get emotional." Madeline fans back tears.

"Would you like to speak to Melody?"

"Yes. Is she nearby?"

Seconds later, Melody's sweet and giggly voice answers. "Hello," she sings into the receiver.

"You are my favorite girl in the whole wide world. How's your day so far?" Madeline tells her.

"Lola and I took a lot of pictures, and we went to feed the ducks. Oh, and Lola painted my nails." Her voice bubbles with excitement.

"What color are your nails?"

"Pink," Melody answers.

"I love it. Give yourself a big hug for me. Can you do that?"

"I don't know. It's kind of hard when I'm holding the phone."

Madeline chuckles. "After you get off, okay?"

"Okay."

"I love you. Where's Lola?"

"Bye, Mommy. I love you too."

Seconds later, Judy picks up. Madeline gives her the number of the hotel and her room number. "Enjoy the show. I love you, Judy."

"I love you, too. Before you go, I had a talk with my son, and I told him he should be proud of you."

"Thank you, Judy."

"I'll tell him to call," Judy says.

She ends the call feeling somewhat better. Madeline reads over an itinerary for the London performances. She feels antsy, anxious. Ten minutes pass, and the phone doesn't ring. Judy did say they were getting ready to leave. Maybe he'll call once they return. New York is five hours behind, which means it'll be five a.m. in London before she hears from him again. The first performance is scheduled for tomorrow night, which gives her a day of rest and some rehearsal before the first show, which starts at eight p.m.

Upon awakening, she immediately checks the phone for messages. There are none. It's now three a.m. in New Jersey. She dials the number to their home, and for a minute it rings continuously. She hangs up and immediately pages him. Still, no response from JB.

Later she meets Gilda for breakfast downstairs.

"You and JB talked?" Gilda asks.

"No."

"Why not?"

"He's unavailable. I talked to Judy, and I told her to have him call me as soon as he could."

Gilda smooths a table napkin across her lap. "I always gave JB the benefit of the doubt. Who do you think took those photos? What did they hope to accomplish? Has anybody else from the family approached JB asking for money?"

"I only know of a handful of them. His family is huge on both sides."

"How is his relationship with them now?"

"Amicable as far as I know."

"Didn't you tell me once that he threatened to cut his father off if he didn't stop asking him for money?"

"He did. It got contemptuous at one point."

"Remember the ex-girlfriend JB was involved with? Whatever happened to her?"

Madeline remembers Basha, JB's ex-girlfriend, along with two others—one was her obstetrician's nurse and Basha's cousin–who were charged in connection with burglarizing and vandalizing Madeline's townhome when she lived in Santa Monica. She believes Basha stole her mother's pearl necklace, too.

"I don't know."

"You think she could be behind this?"

"There's a strong possibility. In the meantime, JB and I are taking the owners of the building to court for breach of contract. In it, they stated the building had state-of-the-art security, not to mention we had a door attendant. However, the cameras weren't on the day the envelope was left at our door and the door attendant doesn't recall events of that day."

"Go figure."

"Not only did they expose JB, but they exposed me, too," Madeline tells her.

The expression in Gilda's eyes fills with questions and concerns.

"Remember last year when I told you I had the flu?"

"You were lethargic and out of it for a couple of weeks there."

"It wasn't the flu."

"No?"

"It turns out I was pregnant, and I..." Madeline covers her face. Gilda notices a new princess-cut diamond wedding set on her ring finger. It sparkles under the restaurant's lights.

Madeline can't stand to see the look of disappointment on Gilda's face. Gilda is an independent thinker, but when it comes to matters such as these, she stands by her convictions. Gilda shares her husband's beliefs: *Life is precious, and it has a purpose.*

"We don't have to talk about this," Gilda tells her.

Madeline dabs at her tears with her table napkin. Gilda takes her hand and squeezes it.

"Look at me," she tells Madeline, but Madeline refuses.

Gilda gives her minutes to compose herself. "I thought it was for the best," Madeline utters.

"I take it at the time you didn't tell JB, but he eventually found out."

"Whoever took the photos of JB and Lilly took photos of me leaving the clinic."

Gilda, still squeezing her hand, says, "I wish I didn't know this. I won't say a word about it to Eugene."

"I hope you understand. I didn't want to—" She sobs into her table napkin.

Gilda signals a waiter for the check. Gilda, still holding her hand, needs to get Madeline's head in a good space for tomorrow night's performance, and she knows just how to do it.

Eleven

JB is headed to Chicago and fully prepared for the backlash from the New Jersey fans. He can take it. Just like he can take subtle digs from Chicago's star player.

"Today we're playing from the tips—twenty grand a hole," the star player tells JB before teeing up. "That's chump change for us. You endorse men's underwear—figured we'd lower it to give you a shot."

"Oh, don't do me any special favors," JB responds.

"Once you've filled your pockets with sneakers and pop money, you've graduated to the big leagues. In the meantime, watch and learn." The star player swings, sending the ball sailing over a fairway of bent grass. Two other players tee up—one is the chief executive officer of a Fortune 500 company based in Chicago; the other a future teammate from the Chicago team. JB watches as they tee up and swing. He's next.

"What's up, Drawers," the star player rags, giving JB a nickname because of the product JB endorses.

JB tees up for the drive. "I'll show you better than I can tell you." With a swing, the ball coasts mid-air before landing a few feet away from the intended hole.

"Lucky. Pretty motherfucker." The star player quotes a line from the movie New Jack City.

"Must be the drawers," JB replies, getting a laugh from the others. The golf game and banter continued into late evening. After freshening up at the hotel, he meets with the star player, the CEO and the other teammate at Smith & Wollensky steakhouse. Dinner is followed with a trip to an exclusive strip club. There, he smokes cigars, sips cognac, and watches two exotic dancers both wearing only G strings and gladiator-style stiletto open-toe boots, engage him in a sensuous lap dance. En Vogue's version of "Giving Him Something He Can Feel" plays as one dancer launches into a handstand. JB watches her legs slowly spread open. A second dancer saunters around his chair. In the dim red-lit room, JB follows her gaze. In one swift move, her thigh drapes over his shoulder. It brushes against his cheek. His gaze now rests on the movement of the first dancer, now circling her hips on his lap. The second dancer takes his face in her hands and turns his head so that he's now looking into her eyes. Her gaze is hypnotic, and he's been in enough champagne rooms to know the routine. In the past—before Madeline—a dancer's hypnotic gaze and body could stimulate pressure points to all corners of his body. Tonight, he's feeling something that he doesn't want to feel—not with her and not with the other dancer. The excitement wears off just as quickly as it emerges.

***

He leaves Chicago the next morning and flies to Detroit to hang out with Caleb, his best friend and Madeline's first cousin. They check out a concert featuring hip-hop artists and follow it up with an after party that doesn't end until four-thirty in the morning. Caleb, still wild and restless, comes home with a girl. JB crashes in an upstairs guest bedroom. Hours later, when he awakens, his head feels like a ton of bricks. The girl who came home with Caleb is now in bed kissing and rubbing him.

"What the fuck—" Startled and disoriented, JB leaps out of the bed, his adrenaline fueled, his nerves rattled when he sees her naked body. A satisfying smirk crosses her lips, "I'm your biggest fan. I've been following your games."

"How did you get in here?"

"I heard when you're a professional athlete, doors tend to open for you literally," she says, fluffing the pillow.

"Get out of here." His tone slices through the air like a dagger.

Her eyes, once flirty and seductive, now bore the weight of his anger. "You don't have to say it like that. Don't you find all this sexy?" She's stretched across the bed with her back arched and breasts protruding like a nude model holding a pose for a painting.

"Out. I'm not playing games," JB says, while watching her rise from the bed still totally naked. Her walk is a sultry dance. "We had fun last night." She winks before walking out of the room. JB slams the door and does a careful inspection of the bed, searching for bodily fluids. Her scent—a rich mixture of floral and Zest–still lingers on the bed sheets and throughout the room. He sits, jogging his memory to what led to this. He had a couple of beers and vodka shots. He was exhausted from all the activities, and every-thing seemed like a blur. He and Madeline aren't on the best of terms, but in no way is he reverting to his wild, partying ways. If he were still at USC, the situation with the girl in the bedroom would've played out much differently. Nowadays, he doesn't trust these women as far as his fade-away jumper.

He walks downstairs and stops at Caleb's bedroom door, which is slightly ajar. He taps lightly, but there's no answer. JB taps louder. Still no answer. He opens the door to find Caleb alone, naked and sprawled across the bed.

JB walks in and kicks Caleb's foot. "Wake your ass up."

"What?" Caleb's eyelids flutter. He's now awake, but groggy.

"When I woke up, your girl was in my bed."

That news stirs Caleb fully awake now to the point he's scrambling, trying to gather his bearings. "Why was she in your bed?"

"Ask her."

The toilet flushes, followed by the sound of water flowing from the bathroom faucet. The door opens, and the girl appears wearing Caleb's oversized jersey. Part of it hangs off her shoulder. Her gaze meets theirs.

"Why were you upstairs in my homeboy's bed?" Caleb asks.

"Blame it on the alcohol. I thought it was your room," she tells him with a straight face.

Caleb and JB exchange looks at the absurdity of her statement.

"Say no more. I'll help find your clothes. Leave my jersey. I'm calling you a cab," Caleb barks before putting on a pair of boxers. Next, he gathers all her belongings and shoves them into her hands.

She frowns in disbelief at him and JB, "You're kicking me out? Caleb, you're tripping."

She drops her clothing and casually removes Caleb's jersey. JB quickly turns his head and walks out. He hears them arguing as he walks down the hall and returns upstairs to the guest room. Once inside, he sits on the edge of the bed trying to remember last night and what led to this morning.

I didn't do anything with her. I don't think I did anything with her.

The house is quiet for some time with no rumblings of Caleb and the girl arguing. Once downstairs, JB notices Caleb's bedroom door is open, and he discovers him lying back in bed.

"Yo, bringing random chicks to your crib is bad business," JB tells him when he enters.

"I know her," Caleb mumbles into the pillow.

"I swear I didn't hear her get in the bed."

"Don't sweat it. I won't tell Maddie." Caleb grins.

"You are trippin,' but seriously though, I don't remember much about last night. And this morning she was all over me."

Caleb's expression turns serious. "All over you *how?*"

"She was kissing me. I was half asleep, and I felt her lips, and for a minute, I thought it was Maddie. When I opened my eyes, her brown complexion and wild morning hair reminded me of Basha."

"Basha? Ol' girl you used to kick it with? Is she still in jail?"

"Don't know. She could rot in hell for all I care."

JB looks around Caleb's room. It's a typical NBA player's bachelor pad. The ceiling and walls are all mirrors. A built-in aquarium with exotic fish is positioned right above the fireplace. The furnishings are all contemporary—marble and onyx.

"Get up so I can kick your ass in Street Fighter," JB tells him.

"Nigga, please," Caleb replies.

"What's for breakfast? I'm starving."

"You're the cook."

"But I'm the guest," JB counters.

"Whip up something."

"Whip these nuts," JB says, and it feels like he's back in the locker room bantering with his old teammate.

In the kitchen, JB finds a carton of eggs and a box of pancake mix inside the refrigerator. He finishes right before noon with a spread big enough to feed himself, Caleb and maybe a few other people. They find seats in Caleb's entertainment room and play Street Fighter II while stopping at certain points to eat.

"JB, the family man," Caleb notes. "How long have you and my cousin been married?"

"Four years."

"Dang. All the hell raising we did, still can't fathom you've settled down."

JB's handling the controls, focusing on the images on the screen. "Maddie rocked my world, and when Melody came along, life took on a whole new, different meaning."

"Sounds inspiring, but I don't see it happening for me *no* time soon. All these beautiful women out here, I won't settle with just one. I need one for every day of the week."

JB remembers their earlier years at USC—their fraternity parties on campus, the away games, how girls sometimes waited hours in hotels for them to arrive.

"Play on, player," JB says before sipping from a can of Budweiser beer. "Turned in my player card. To my surprise, it wasn't hard. With Maddie, I've made a fresh start. She forever holds the key to my heart."

"Cupid missed my heart and went straight for my brain. Falling in love at this point is utterly insane. She could be fine as Janet Jackson and sexy as Lela Rochon. There'll be a different girl out there who'll always turn me on," Caleb answers.

JB chuckles while still working the controls to the video game. "And when you finally do decide to settle down, life will be sweet."

"Shit. It's sweet now."

"Look at us. Remember how we used to sit at your crib and play Zelda all night, talking about the money we'd make playing ball?" JB asks, handling the controls.

"Word."

"My people think I'm a bank," JB tells him.

"Put your foot down."

"I take it you don't have those problems."

"First off, I don't have a million-dollar deal and an underwear endorsement," Caleb tells him.

"Everybody wants something—from Pops to family I haven't dealt with in ages."

"Pops is a given. Think of all the time and money he invested in you."

"Like you said earlier, I'm putting my foot down. I'm putting the brakes on him. No more money to purchase investment property until I start seeing some returns."

"Look on the bright side: It could be worse. I know niggas on the team whose salary goes to child support, paternity suits, alimony—in some cases, all three."

"Won't ever see me in that predicament." JB puts down the controller.

"Why'd you stop?" Caleb looks confused.

"I'm just jogging my memory. You've blacked out before, and people told you things that happened that you had no recollection of."

"Usually happens after I've had several drinks. I do remember last night—afterward, my ass slept like a baby—until you woke me up."

"Any broad that intentionally comes to their boyfriend's best friend's room, crawls in bed with him and feels him up can't be trusted."

"You had a lot to drink," Caleb says to him after a moment of silence, "but I wouldn't think you'd do anything with her."

The thought makes JB quiver. The sudden uneasiness is something he must settle.

* * *

"Get your shit and get out," the owner of the basement apartment where Basha rents barks at her.

"But I was going to pay you tomorrow."

"I need you out. I've got a new occupant moving in tomorrow."

"Can I at least freshen up?"

"Out. Now." The owner shoves a notice at her. Basha takes and crumbles it.

Her job as a fashion photographer's assistant and freelance photography barely keep her afloat. *Give it up. Go back to L.A.* She hasn't seen JB or Madeline entering or leaving their apartment building for some time. She saw a moving truck days after having dropped off the pictures. She wonders if they moved. She frequents the public library reading newspapers and sports magazines. She doesn't own a television, so she has no way of watching ESPN to see if there's mention of JB. She has a stack of old sports magazines that have either featured JB on the cover or have showcased an article about him. A couple of years ago, there was a story about him in Ebony magazine, balancing life as a young professional athlete and a family man. The article mentioned a home in suburban New Jersey—to determine just where in New Jersey was a shot in the dark.

He's never respected you; he used you for his benefit, yet you continue stalking him. Admit it to yourself, you are sick. You and Rachael spent three lousy months in jail because you wanted to destroy him. Joke's on you.

Now her friend Rachael doesn't answer her calls or return her letters, angry still for her involvement in a situation that left a permanent blemish on her record.

"All this, was it worth it?" Rachael asked.

Basha couldn't give her an answer. It was their last conversation.

Shortly afterward, Basha went to her parents' home in Leimert Park to retrieve the stolen saltwater pearl necklace hidden inside the pocket of an old USC jacket JB had given her. She recalls the gesture. It was particularly chilly that late night on campus. He took off his jacket and draped it across her shoulders. Crazy how she can reminisce details of moments spent with him. Her heart still flutters when she remembers his kisses, the late nights they spent "studying," the rare occasions when they got spontaneous. They'd jump in his father's early 1980s Porsche and drive to the street where his parents lived. There, he'd park, and they'd watch the city lights. Views from Baldwin Hills were usually better than those from Hollywood before the action inside caused the windows to fog.

The Ebony article featured a photograph of the family sitting in front of a piano. Madeline plays, yet she gazes admiringly at his face. JB appears to be singing and playing with their daughter who sits on his lap. The caption reads: *Family time cherished with wife of two years, Madeline, and their two-year-old daughter, Melody.*

She wonders if they discovered the photos. The quiet and uncertainty has her anxious. She sometimes stands across the street from Lilly's apartment building with her camera hoping to see something. Lilly was another girl who happened to be in JB's life while Basha and JB were together. She stumbled upon them sitting on a park bench while exploring Central Park, scouting out locations for fashion photos. Neither of them noticed her. She followed them traipsing the sidewalks. Lilly had long goddess locs, wore a Japanese kimono with black Doc Martens boots. JB sported Adidas athletic gear. Their styles couldn't be more opposite—a total contrast. He towered over her, yet there was something about them that screamed, *There's more to it than meets the eye.*

When Basha arrives inside the studio where she works, Crystal Waters' "Gypsy Woman" blares from a stereo's speakers. The photographer whom she assists is in the middle of a fashion photo shoot. His subjects are a pair of angular, swan-like models posing against a backdrop of cascading silk. She's relieved he's in the middle of a shoot and no one from the receptionist downstairs to other members of the photographer's staff questions why she's pulling two large suitcases stuffed to capacity with all her belongings. Rushing to get out of the apartment, she didn't get an opportunity to freshen up. She finds her toiletry kit, rushes to the nearest restroom, and locks the door.

A toilet flushes, and seconds later, a tall, racially ambiguous girl sporting a messy ponytail walks to the sink to wash her hands. She examines her makeup before her eyes connect with Basha's.

"I know you," Basha tells her.

The girl pinches her nostrils and sniffs. Soon, blood pours from her nose.

Basha hurries to grab tissue from inside a stall. The girl takes it and pinches her nose, resting her elbows on the sink.

"Thanks," she manages to say.

"Like I said earlier, I've seen you before," Basha says. "You're from L.A."

She flashes a sideways glance at Basha from behind the tissues before removing them to speak. "How did you guess?"

"I'm from L.A., Leimert Park."

"Nice" is the girl's response before she covers her nose.

Basha frowns. "Do I need to call for help?"

"It's okay," she declares. "I'm fine." She throws away a bloody tissue before grabbing a new one.

Basha retrieves a toothbrush and travel-size toothpaste from inside her toiletry kit.

"On second thought, I might need your help," the girl says to Basha.

Basha studies her. She's wearing a designer, but Basha doesn't remember who. Her shoes are Manolo Blahnik. Basha recognizes them from a Vogue magazine fashion spread she saw in the public library.

"What's your name?" she asks.

"Basha."

"I'm Mona. I fibbed when I said I didn't need you to call for help."

Basha notices her sweating. "I'm calling 9-1-1," Basha tells her before dashing out of the restroom.

Twelve

The curtain rises, and the lighting inside the Barbican Center gives the illusion of sunrise. Madeline strikes the keys of the black grand Steinway piano, swift yet deftly. Lynnwood stands at the podium conducting the orchestra. As cellos and violins play, the lights onstage become warmer, and the sound of the orchestra coincides with the mood of the lighting. Madeline focuses on the notes, making sure she hits the right points. Lynnwood opens the performance with her "Sunset Composition," a piece inspired by her mother's love of sunsets. If her mother were alive, Madeline imagines her sitting in the front row, radiant in kelly green with diamonds sparkling in each ear. The piece is nine minutes long, and when it ends, the orchestra immediately segues into several more songs, and nearly two hours later, the audience is standing and applauding when Lynnwood takes Madeline's hand, and together, they bow. He then motions her to walk forward, and she bows again. Her heart races when the applause from the audience heightens, and she hears them cheering.

When she exits the stage, standing there along with Gilda is her father, Aunt Mary, Judy, and Melody. She stops in her tracks and covers her mouth. Tears flow. She can't believe her eyes. She picks up Melody and holds her close.

"Wow," Madeline cries, a bit overwhelmed by the sudden rush of adrenaline. "You're so beautiful. Did you see Mommy?"

The applause is deafening. Backstage the family gathers in a green room. While holding Melody's hand, Madeline converses with countless faces offering praises on the performance. She looks and sees her father, Eugene, conversing with Lynnwood. She leaves Melody with Judy before she joins them.

"Lynnwood, did you know my family was coming?"

"Had no clue, but I wished I could've gotten off the stage sooner, so I could've seen the look on your face," Lynnwood tells her.

"Hopefully, someone captured the moment. It was magical." She turns to her father. "Your presence means so much to me."

"I am grateful for the opportunity, baby girl. Music has the power to bring people together. I pray you two see eye-to-eye on the creative aspects."

Madeline and Lynnwood nod and look away, seeing how sometimes they clash on ideas and concepts.

"What I like about us is that we can agree to disagree," Lynnwood states.

"Most of the time," Madeline says.

"But big brother Lynn is always right," Lynnwood says with a smirk.

"Maybe forty percent of the time," Madeline adds.

Lynnwood holds up his hands. "I'll relent this evening." He excuses himself. Eugene then turns to Madeline. "Smart man," he says. "Didn't he go to Juilliard?"

"Yes."

"Did he graduate?"

"No."

"Well, it doesn't matter. It doesn't take away from his accomplishments. I've always prayed for God's hand to guide you in the right direction and link you with those who will position you to greatness."

"You don't think I could've done it on my own?"

"That's not what I meant—" Eugene says.

He studies her for a beat. He's debating whether to discuss the photos that were mailed to his church in an envelope with no return address. The sender mailed them from a post office in New York City. The atmosphere is lively, and Madeline appears happy. Coming forward with this will probably shift the dynamics of the tour. An internal war rages: *Reveal what he saw in the* photos or *remain quiet and stay out of Madeline's affairs.*

* * *

Judy gives Madeline an envelope. It is thick, and when Madeline finds alone time, she opens it to reveal notebook pages containing JB's handwriting.

Maddie,

I want to apologize. We should never part and not be on speaking terms. I admit, pride got the best of me. I didn't want to see you go. Now that you've graduated and I'm not going to Barcelona, I wanted us to spend quality time as a family. Three weeks here, and there isn't enough. Melody and I need you. I understand our professions take us in opposite directions, but the separation is too much. You are my refuge from this crazy, mixed-up world. You only require my love and faithfulness, and for the last four years, that's all I've given. To know my reputation and the kind of person I was before you and how you changed all that is nothing short of a miracle. I've honored our vows—for better or worse, to love and cherish you and only you.

Those photos you saw of Lilly and me were just me being a listening ear. The only thing I'm guilty of is not being forthcoming. I promise you all we did was talk, nothing more. I know it doesn't look right, I know it wasn't the ideal thing to do, but it happened, and if I had to do it all over again, I might have taken a different approach.

What upsets me about you is how you make life-changing decisions without first talking it over with me. First, it was the abortion—I still haven't gotten over that, how you could go through with it and continue like nothing happened. It makes me question what other secrets you're keeping. I understand your going on tour is a way to build your notoriety, but again, you didn't tell me until a month or two before the tour started. Don't you think I should've known months in advance? Something you said bothered me—you said your father made you have this baby, and you really didn't want to put me in this situation.

Look, I know what happened between us was unexpected and our lives snowballed, but Melody is a testament of when passionate souls collide, and even if it wasn't planned, she is here, she is our child, and she is beautiful.

I want us to be together, despite the distance and separation. I know there are tough days ahead, but there's one thing for certain: I love you, and true love never fails.

> *There is a sea between you and me*
> *But nothing can separate our love*
> *Heartache spreading all around us*
> *The ground shaking beneath us*
> *The eleventh hour falling upon us*
> *Nothing can separate our love*

She notices two more pages of lyrics, and she reads them while shedding tears and wetting the paper. An overwhelming feeling of guilt consumes her. She has one good cry, and when morning arrives, she shelves her emotions like a librarian shelves a book. The performance goes on without a hitch, no family this time—they flew back to the states. Madeline, Lynnwood, and the orchestra bring the room to its knees before they board a flight to Paris.

***

Madeline dazzles in red when she graces the stage at the Philharmonie de Paris. The spotlight follows her to the shiny black grand piano where she sits and when the applause ceases, she plays the notes to her "Sunset Composition." Lynnwood waves his conductor's baton. In that moment, the beauty of the piece even gives her chills when the rest of the orchestra plays. They perform for nearly two hours before Madeline, Lynnwood and the rest of the orchestra exit the stage to the green room to meet patrons and take photographs

She converses with reporters from a French magazine about the modern landscape of classical music when she feels a tap on her shoulder. She turns and sees her cousin Gracie Turrentine also dressed in red. They scream and embrace as if it's been years instead of a little over a month since they last saw each other.

"I saw on television you and Lynnwood were performing, so I told my boyfriend, 'We're going.' This is the hottest ticket in town," Gracie tells her.

"And did we live up to your expectations?" Madeline asks.

"Cousin, I was crying—literally. I remember the days and hours we poured into our craft, and it's amazing that it didn't take years—it happened to you right away. Your brilliance is undeniable. I recognized it the moment I heard you play at Juilliard."

"What was your boyfriend thinking when he saw you crying?" Madeline asks.

"He thought I was nuts." She laughs. Madeline's dress catches her eye. "This is gorgeous. We're both wearing red."

They stop to pose for a photographer. Madeline's eyes are radiant. Her red, sequined off-shoulder gown accentuates her tiny waist and round hips. Gracie's dress has a plunging neckline revealing a princess-length flower diamond necklace. When the photographer walks away, up walks Gregory Washington III, a piece of a puzzle from Madeline's past, wearing a black Italian-cut suit.

"Honey," Gracie calls.

Madeline's heart races.

Gracie puts her arm around Gregory's waist and brings him closer. "This is my cousin Madeline—pianist, composer extraordinaire."

Madeline and Gregory don't know whether to hug or shake hands.

"I know," he says, looking directly into her eyes. "The cousin part, I didn't." It suddenly awakens the hairs on Madeline's body.

"I am a fan of his mother's. She is a Broadway legend..." Gracie begins.

"Small world. Gregory and I used to attend summer camp right outside of L.A.," Madeline answers.

"You never told me that," Gracie says to him.

"And why should I?" is his response.

"When I mentioned the concert, you didn't give me a clue that you knew Madeline."

"And again, I ask *why* is that important?" Gregory answers, almost annoyed he's getting pressed about it.

It's been nearly five years since Madeline saw Gregory. Their last exchange was intense. A hint of his cologne creeps into her nostrils, reminding her of moments she'd forgotten. Gone are the designer horn-rimmed glasses he wore from the time they were teens. In his early teens, he was scrawny, prankish, and often annoying. Something strange and unusual happened during the summer of 1987. Gregory's voice got deeper, his shoulders broadened, and his arms gained a little muscle. His attitude became mellow, though hints of his mischievousness seeped out from time to time. He became a good kisser breath always tasted like he managed to quickly and discreetly pop in a mint. Looking at him now standing next to Gracie, his skin is the color of toasted chestnuts. The expression in his eyes is smoldering—either that or they're still adjusting to life without the bifocals.

"Did you enjoy the show?" Madeline asks him. *Such a loaded question.*

"I managed to stay awake," he quips.

Madeline covers her smile—memories of a concert he'd taken her to, and the image of him falling asleep in the middle of a performance by the great concert pianist, Martha Austin.

"Did I miss something?" Gracie asks.

"I'm amazed. It's a small world," Madeline answers.

"Gregory and I met at a dinner party. His mother and my grandmother had a mutual friend who was the host. Why were we sitting in a corner, low-key cracking jokes at the guests?"

Madeline glances at Gregory who looks away. His hands are inside his pockets.

"He makes me laugh. I think it's sexy," Gracie says, bringing him closer.

Madeline nods, never thinking she'd run into Gracie and Gregory, and certainly not both—together.

"Whatever happened to Rome and your opportunity with the opera house?" Madeline asks.

"I never made it. I flew into Nice, and it's been nice ever since," Gracie says.

"Please explain." Madeline is curious.

"I awake to amazing views of the Mediterranean. I wish you would come and hang out with us," Gracie gushes.

Madeline glances at Gregory. If she had chosen to stay with Gregory, life with him in the South of France would consist of days creating music in rooms with views of the Mediterranean. Gregory loved yachting, so there would be days sailing on the Riviera. He loved exotic sports cars like Lamborghinis and Ferraris, so cruising the promenade with the top down would be an everyday affair. If she remembers correctly, he was being groomed to run his father's multi-million-dollar company. Then she remembers why life with Gregory wouldn't work.

"I almost forgot: I've got an interview with some journalists who are here from New York," Madeline says.

"Awesome. What are you doing tomorrow?" Gracie asks.

"Sound check. Shouldn't last long."

"Gregory and I are at the Ritz adjacent to the Place Vendome. Let's have lunch there around noon."

"That would be awesome. Gregory, are you coming?" Madeline asks.

"Only if you want me to," Gregory answers.

Madeline catches the double entendre. Gregory notices her slight eye roll. He's hoping Gracie doesn't see it.

"Let the cousins have our moment," Gracie says, taking his hand.

"Cousins. Wow." Gregory shakes his head. The fact seems mind blowing.

Madeline watches them walk in the crowded room with Gracie leading Gregory by the hand. She notices him take one last glance at her with that smoldering look in his eyes.

The room babbles in French. The two journalists who've flown in from New York have set up an area for Madeline and Lynnwood to interview. Madeline notices Lynnwood appear from another section of the room with traces of lipstick kisses on both of his cheeks.

"That's quite an admirer," Madeline says to Lynnwood.

"What are you talking about?" he asks.

Madeline reaches over to wipe his cheeks. His skin is soft to her touch. He reaches inside his jacket to retrieve a handkerchief to wipe away the lipstick traces.

"Some get carried away with the cheek kissing," Lynnwood explains.

"I think they like you."

"Oui, *oui*." Lynnwood replies.

"Tell us how this collaboration came about," the first interviewer says.

Lynnwood glances at his watch. "I'll give you the Reader's Digest version," he begins. "I had this idea of tapping into my classical roots for some time, and I decided to take an inspirational route back to Juilliard, where I honed my musical chops. I think it was a year or so ago, I saw this young lady performing a recital piece, and she blew me away."

The second interviewer asks, "What was it about her performance that gave you that reaction?"

"The complexity of the arrangement, all the details we composers notice when we hear a piece that resonates with our soul," Lynnwood responds.

The second interviewer then asks Madeline, "Did you know he was in the audience?"

"No," is Madeline's reply.

The first interviewer asks, "How did you know the moment that you wanted to collaborate with her?"

Lynnwood takes a deep breath. "I don't say this about a lot of people, but listening to her skills—the dexterity and proficiency of her delivery—is almost like listening to myself. The minute I heard her, I knew right away that I wanted to collaborate with her."

Madeline turns to Lynnwood. "Really?" she asks.

The interviewers notice Madeline's reaction. The first interviewer asks, "How does it feel to have one of the biggest names in jazz and classical music say this about you?"

Madeline puts a hand over her heart. "I learn something new every day." She turns to Lynnwood. "I'm honored to be handpicked by you."

Lynnwood shrugs it off like it's no big deal. The interviewers continue with their questions to the point, Lynnwood starts nodding off.

The following day, Madeline enters the Ritz where Gracie stands awaiting her arrival. They greet each other with a cheek kiss before sitting at a table with a view.

"I couldn't wait to get the opportunity to talk to you," she says to Madeline.

"Same here."

The dining area inside the Ritz is bright with ornate furniture and décor and an old Parisian charm.

"I want to cut to the chase, because I noticed something," Gracie starts.

Madeline is attentive.

"You knew Gregory from summer camp?"

"Yes," Madeline answers.

"You liked each other?"

"He had a crush on me," Madeline answers.

"I see," Gracie responds.

"I'll tell you everything you want to know," Madeline says.

Gracie sighs, debating if she wants to hear it. After leaving the event last night with Gregory, she noticed how unusually quiet he had become. "What are the odds, I'm with someone who used to like my cousin?"

"It's a small world," Madeline answers.

"When did you first meet Gregory?"

"I think I was twelve. Camp lasted about two weeks in June. My father insisted I go. I met people who I am friends with to this day."

"Anything happened between you and Gregory while at camp?"

"No. It was later–Like the summer when I was seventeen. After high school graduation things started happening between us."

"How long did it last?" Gracie asks.

"Just for the summer, and when I look back, Gregory was away at sea half that summer, so it was really a few weeks, if that."

"Were you intimate?"

"We were," Madeline answers. She notices Gracie's shoulders sinking as she lowers her face.

"Gracie, there were things that complicated my relationship with Gregory."

Gracie's eyes meet hers.

"Well, that same summer, weeks before Gregory and I were intimate, I was also intimate with JB while Gregory was away at sea."

Gracie met JB once. She even attended one of his basketball games with Madeline.

Madeline continues, "In my defense, I didn't hear from Gregory. I didn't know if he had forgotten about me or if we would ever see each other. I got no phone calls, no letters. I didn't know what to expect. That's when JB and I grew extremely close."

"Sounds like something out of a novel," Gracie responds.

"Yes. A romance and a thriller all rolled into one," Madeline says.

Gracie doesn't respond.

"What about you? What about the offer with the opera house in Rome?"

Gracie sighs. "I got with Gregory and lost track."

Madeline shakes her head. "Gracie. Was he worth it?"

Gracie takes a moment before she answers. "Yes."

Thirteen

Bo Young of Valor Limo greets JB when he arrives at LAX, taking JB's luggage and loading it into the trunk of a Land Cruiser SUV. JB never forgot during the riots, how Bo's limo service was the only company willing to drive the distance from John Wayne Airport in Santa Ana to the front door of his parents' house in Baldwin Hills.

Sitting in the backseat, JB contemplates whether to tell his father the news of his move to Chicago or allow him to be surprised like everyone else. As before, Bo drops off JB at his parents' front door and unloads his luggage, even taking it inside. JB gives him a crisp one-hundred-dollar bill.

"I got your card. Never worry about me not calling," JB tells him before they shake hands.

Just as Bo leaves, JB's pager sounds off. He looks at the code. It's Aaron Levy, his agent. He sees Smitty's tail wagging, and he opens the slide door. The energetic Ibizan Hound is on its hind legs. JB kneels to pet him; the dog licks his face. He checks his food and water bowls. James or Judy must've filled them before they took off. He was hoping to see his daughter and spend some quality time with her. He changes into shorts and a shirt to take Smitty for a short walk. He scrolls his pager to see a page from Madeline. She's nine hours ahead in Paris. He has her itinerary and thinks of catching a flight to surprise her.

During the flight to L.A., he opened one of his composition notebooks to jot down lyrics:

What I wouldn't do
To be sleeping next to you
I'll fly Mach 2.0
Even sail the ocean blue

When he returns home, he calls the contact number she gave him, and it rings continuously before JB is prompted to leave a message.

"I just wanted to hear your voice. I love you," he says before hanging up.

He scrolls his pager to see numbers from Anna, his father, Lilly, the Rap Mogul, and his friend, Paul. He calls his agent.

"What up? What up?" JB begins the call.

"Press conference to announce the trade is scheduled two days from now."

"I'm in L.A. Where do you need me?" JB asks.

"Stay. L.A. is perfect."

"I'm looking forward to this move."

"I understand. Listen, reps from Gatorade want you as the face of their product."

"Make that happen," JB says just as another page goes off. He looks and notices the code is from Anna.

"I'm busy, you're busy. Time is money. If it's not making dollars, it's not making sense," Aaron says before he and JB end their call.

He gets off the call with Aaron and finds a comfortable spot on the couch to call Anna. She answers on the third ring.

"It's your big bad wolf," he says.

"I just got off the phone with Paul, and he said you were coming to L.A.," she says.

"I'm here. I was about to call you."

"Sure."

"I swear."

"Anyway, tonight I'm hosting a gathering. I've invited you, Paul, and a few other friends. I'll kick things off around eight."

"I'm coming through."

"We're celebrating power moves," she says.

"I'll see you then."

The minute JB emerges from behind the wheel of a brand-new red Porsche 911, he hears music thumping, lively chatter, and laughter. Inside, the noise intensifies with revelers mingling and dancing. JB enters slapping high fives, dapping, and bantering with familiar faces. Paul, his friend, and fraternity brother, greets him with a secret handshake and a hug.

"Feels like we're back on the yard," he tells Paul.

JB notices other brothers from the fraternity. Their voices are loud enough they drown out the music. A DJ mixes tunes on a turntable that gets JB, Paul and the other fraternity brothers percolating. Soon, JB breaks into a chant while the other brothers follow suit. The dancing and strolling has JB sweating, and without a second thought, he takes off his shirt. A couple of the other brothers do the same. Once finished, they slap high fives and handshakes.

Walking through the crowded room, JB notices more familiar faces, among them the youngest sibling of an internationally known pop star family. Paul introduces them.

"I know you," she says to JB in a soft voice. Her iconic smile dazzles.

JB guesses her to be five-feet-three, the same height as Madeline. Her hair is styled into long box braids, and her eyes travel from the distinct and intricate formation of his abdominals to the ringlets crowning his head. She gives JB the shirt he tossed aimlessly about.

"Boxers or briefs?" she asks, watching him don his shirt.

Normally he has a catchy one-liner response, but this pop phenomenon has him momentarily speechless. He notices a simple gold wedding band on her ring finger. He looks around the room.

"Where's your husband?" he asks. "Because what I'm about to say may not be appropriate."

"Oh, boy." Paul chuckles. "When I pledged undergrad, he was my big brother," Paul explains to her. "We called him Wolf."

"Wolf?" she says. "Wow. What big hands you have." She takes his hands, noticing his wedding band.

"Big enough to palm round objects with, my dear," JB responds.

"Oooh. What nice, firm muscles you have," she goes on.

"Listen Little Red Riding Hood," Paul interrupts, "go before you both get in trouble."

"Can she at least get to the part about my teeth?" JB asks.

She laughs. "It was a pleasure to meet you," she says to JB.

JB takes her hand and kisses it. "It's a pleasure to meet me too," he says and winks.

Both he and Paul watch her saunter and mingle with the rest of the revelers.

"That's you, bruh?" JB asks, his eyes are still fixed on her.

"No," Paul answers. "We're in the middle of filming. She's the lead in a project I'm directing. I can't say much, but the shit is epic."

"Can't wait to see it. She got sex scenes?"

"She's still America's sweetheart. We got to keep her aesthetic wholesome."

"No titties? No ass?"

Paul emphatically shakes his head. "Your girl Lilly tried it. See what happened to her career."

A tall, attractive model type with golden brown skin, wearing a flowing sundress slides next to Paul, giving him a kiss on the cheek. She's a natural beauty—face doesn't have a trace of makeup. Her smile is warm and carefree.

"My girl, Tori," Paul says to JB.

"What a pretty name. It's fitting," JB tells her.

"JB, let me guess: James?" Tori says to him.

"That's my Pops' name," JB answers.

"I've been wondering the same thing," Paul begins. "What does JB stand for?"

"Just Baaad," JB responds with a straight face.

Paul shakes his head. "You wild, bruh."

He and JB do their secret handshake and lean in for a hug before Paul takes Tori's hand.

Minutes later, JB steps outside for a walk on the terrace. The nighttime air in L.A. is brisk, and the heat from a nearby fire pit is welcoming like a jacket draped over one's shoulder. Anna, the pop artist, and others sit before the fire pit. Anna holds an unlit cigarette. JB sits between Anna and another attractive female whom he recognizes but can't remember where or how. She's wearing a Yves Saint Laurent pantsuit; her hair is pulled into a bun. She has a stately aura about her. It reminds him of Madeline. Anna introduces her to JB.

"Gadise Tesfaye," Anna tells him. "She's a filmmaker extraordinaire who's worked with Paul and other industry giants."

"You went to 'SC?" JB asks.

"Yes. I was in film school from '88 to '90," Gadise tells him.

"I left in '88."

"You graduate?" she asks.

"No. I dropped out and turned pro," JB tells her.

"I see."

"You live in L.A.?" he asks.

"Yes," she answers.

"Where are you from?"

"Addis Ababa. My father was a government official, so my family moved often. We lived in Italy, Switzerland, London, New York City."

"You watch sports?" he asks.

"Just soccer. My youngest brother plays for Italy."

"What's his name?"

"Menab Tesfaye."

"That's your brother?"

"You know him?" Her eyes light up.

"The Pelé of Italé."

She smiles. JB notices how it radiates. The light from the fire pit casts sparkles in her eyes.

"You get to see him in action?" JB asks.

"I'm afraid I don't."

"Why not."

"I'm always busy."

"Doing what?"

"Running my company."

JB notices she isn't wearing a ring. He glances across the way to see the pop superstar he met earlier cuddled up next to a gentleman who's whispering in her ear. Her smile resembles a young girl discovering the joys of courting for the first time.

"Anna mentioned you're a filmmaker. Have I seen your work?" JB asks.

"I've produced and directed several movies and documentaries. I co-produced Paul's movie."

"We were still at 'SC when he started writing the script," JB tells her.

"Paul's movie was riveting with a deep message. I told him if he keeps writing and directing projects like that, I'll be one hundred percent behind him."

"That's dope," JB says.

"You never told me what you do," she says.

"What do you mean? You don't know?"

"You said you dropped out to go pro. It's safe to assume you play basketball."

"Are you for real?"

"Other than soccer, I'm clueless when it comes to sports."

"Do you at least read the newspapers, watch a little television?"

"I work constantly. I rarely get time to sit. Honestly, this is the longest I've sat and had a conversation that didn't involve movie bids or offers."

JB taps Anna who's busy talking to the gentleman next to her. "Excuse me," he says to her. "She asked what I did for a living."

Anna looks at Gadise and smiles cunningly. "She's just fibbing."

"I honestly didn't know," Gadise explains. Her expression seems to align with her words.

"Where were you when he was at 'SC?" Anna asks Gadise.

"I told her I had already moved on when she came along," JB tells Anna.

"Well, Gaddie, if you must know..." Anna begins.

"Hold up. What did you just call her?" JB says to Anna.

"Gaddie," Anna answers.

"Gaddie?" JB asks, as if he needs clarification.

"Yes. My friends call me Gaddie," Gadise answers.

JB chuckles. "My wife's name is Madeline, and we call her Maddie."

"Gaddie, Maddie, Maddie, Gaddie." Anna puts her arm around JB and brings him closer. "He's one of the leading scorers in the NBA. He's an Olympic medalist, but most importantly, he is my ace."

Gadise nods. "Now I know."

The DJ spins the latest hits along with R&B classics that get the crowd up and dancing.

"Let's dance," JB tells Gadise.

"I'm not that good," she answers.

"Just follow my lead," he whispers.

She notices other couples slow dancing. She looks into his eyes. He's a heartthrob with handsome features, winsome lips, and dark, penetrable eyes. She didn't come to catch. Anna Palermo's parties are where you come to network, not hook up. Besides, he's married. She wraps her arms around him, following his lead. The song ends, but they continue to hold each other close before JB finally pulls away.

"I think I'd better say good night," he tells her.

"Me too."

They part and go their separate ways but somehow find themselves minutes later outside getting into their respective vehicles. No words exchange, just furtive glances. She starts up the engine to her Mercedes convertible; he revs up the engine of his Porsche and drives off downhill in the direction of the lights twinkling below.

Fourteen

Basha called Mona's sister, Anna, four days ago. She finally shows up at Mona's apartment.

"Let's step into my office," Anna tells Basha. She follows Anna outside to the fire escape landing of Mona's Chelsea apartment. Anna lights a cigarette and takes a quick drag, "The only reason you're not splattered on the pavement is that you saved my sister's life. Don't think for a minute I forgot." The smoke from her cigarette tickles Basha's nose.

"What are you talking about?"

"Don't play dumb. You know what you did. *You* almost cost my friend his freedom and his livelihood. Understand this: When you fuck with him, you fuck with me."

"I was good to JB, and he never appreciated it."

"Newsflash: He *never* wanted you. You see the problem with girls like you, you think your tits and naughty bits are enough to sustain a man. My dear, your situation ran its course."

Basha shakes her head. "You don't know what you're talking about."

"I'll give it to you straight, no chaser. First night after I saw him play at 'SC, we played a game of one-on-one. It went on all night. You were probably with him then. *Guess what*: I didn't care, and the way he slammed dunked this," she points to herself, "he didn't care about you either."

The more Anna talks, the more Basha wants to toss her over the railing. She is tiny enough for Basha to do just that. Anna takes a drag from her cigarette. "What are you doing in the city?" she asks.

"I'm making it."

"Save the speech. How are you paying the bills?"

"Freelance photography, photographer's assistant," Basha answers.

Anna studies Basha for a minute. She's beautiful, tall, and slender. She notices her father's work when it comes to breast augmentation. Basha's cleavage is vast. "I know those girls had a field day with you."

Basha manages to mentally block out the nearly three-month stint in L.A. County.

"I've spent a night in jail, I know." Anna tosses her cigarette. "Where are you staying?" she asks.

"I was in a basement apartment in Brooklyn—Flatbush."

"What happened?"

"Gigs dried up."

"You're homeless," Anna responds.

Basha never imagined hearing someone say that about her.

"You've got a week here with my sister, after which, you're on your own. I'm still pissed at what you did. You cost JB the first-round draft pick and a soft drink endorsement."

"I didn't lie. She was underage and pregnant."

"You should've kept your mouth closed." She retrieves another cigarette and lights it before taking a drag. A New York City summer breeze rustles generous strands of her neatly trimmed asymmetrical bob. "A major reason he's not with you: your big-assed mouth." She exhales.

"I'm checking on Mona." Basha has had enough of Anna's ranting and her cigarette smoke.

Mona is still in bed when Basha enters her bedroom. Four days ago, Mona was in the emergency room with a perforated septum. According to one of the attending physicians, the hole was bigger than two centimeters. Mona's nose is still bandaged from when the doctors inserted a button to seal the hole.

"I'm not judging. I'm glad I was there to help," Basha says before sitting at the foot of the bed. While Mona was in the ER, Basha searched her wallet for numbers and found a business card with Anna's information.

"Thanks for contacting my sister. My mother would've freaked out," Mona tells her.

"Why wouldn't you want her to know?"

"She tends to overreact, and I wasn't in the mood for it. She's better off in Italy. Don't try to reach out."

And from what Basha gathered in the days after seeing Mona in the restroom, she suspects Mona uses cocaine. As she went through Mona's pocketbook to gather information for the doctor and nurses, she discovered a vial containing white powder. She knew it was cocaine when she placed a little on the tip of her tongue, and it went numb. When she saw Mona's driver's license, she was shocked to learn Mona was just two years younger than her. She looks nothing like the photos that are displayed prominently throughout her apartment. The girl she sees lying in bed in front of her wears the vestiges of nightlife parties on her skinny, chiseled face. Basha imagines she's barely over a hundred pounds—her collar bone is visible and looks like a line is drawn through her pale beige skin, connecting one ball point shoulder to the other.

"You could use a burger," Basha tells her.

"I don't eat red meat or bread," she answers.

"Then what do you eat?"

"Veggie and chicken broth."

"That's it?"

"And drink vodka with my Perrier."

"I'm not judging," Basha continues.

"Of course you are."

"I don't know you." Basha laughs.

"You haven't seen this face in Seventeen, Young Ms., Mademoiselle? You haven't watched me on *The Show* or seen me in music videos?"

Basha points. "Not that face." She giggles.

Mona reaches across the bed and opens her nightstand to retrieve a magazine. Basha notices Mona on the cover. Her face is fuller; her features are delicate and not harsh.

"How old were you when that was taken?"

"Eighteen."

Basha flips open the magazine to look at the rest of Mona's editorial spread. "I love the dress you're wearing," Basha tells her.

"We were debuting Dior's summer collection that year."

"Do you ever get to keep the pieces?"

"Sometimes."

"I love shoes. What size do you wear?" Basha asks.

"An eight."

"Too bad. I wear a ten, sometimes an eleven," Basha tells her.

Anna enters. "I need to speak to my sister in private."

Basha rises from the foot of the bed and enters the living room. She hears Anna firmly closing the door shut behind her. Basha remembers when she and JB were together, Anna was a constant looming presence. What Anna just revealed to her about her one-on-one with JB is triggering. She wonders how his wife deals with Anna. Basha sits on the sofa, and her mind figures plots and scenarios and what-ifs. It's strange how life works. Nothing is coincidence; it's all a divine plan.

Basha thinks, *Maybe this is God's way of getting JB and me to reconnect with each other.* Mona is connected to Anna, and Anna and JB are joined at the hip.

The door opens, and Anna appears. Seeing Basha this close after what happened with JB makes her cautious.

"You're lucky my sister likes you," Anna tells her. "Mona, I'm out," she yells.

"Basha, are you still here?" Mona calls from her bedroom.

Basha appears in her doorway.

Mona sighs. "I'm going insane."

"That makes two of us," Basha responds.

Basha runs frustrated hands through her long, thick, coarse hair. A week seems like a decent amount of time to turn things around. Then again, she was in New York City, and time travels at the speed of light. Hopefully, what she has in mind pays off.

Fifteen

Madeline retreats to the solitude of her dressing room. Tonight's performance, followed up with hobnobbing, pushes her to the point of exhaustion. A sharp knock on the door startles her from her thoughts.

"Go away," she says half-jokingly.

"It's me," Lynnwood announces. "There's someone here who wants to see you."

Madeline looks at her reflection in the mirror. She opens the door, and Lynnwood is there with Martha Austin, classical pianist extraordinaire. Instantly, Madeline's eyes light up upon seeing the legendary pianist.

"We're waiting," Lynnwood says to her.

"Pardon me. This is totally unexpected." Madeline opens the door wide enough for them to enter.

"We're honored to have you," Madeline tells her. "Please, have a seat."

Martha, dressed in a long, black glittery gown sits, her silver-gray hair hangs past her shoulders. "I was impressed, especially knowing this is your first major European tour. I remember my first time performing abroad."

"Thanks for paving the way," Madeline responds.

"I came of age during a time when you had to prove yourself worthy."

"First time I attended your concert; I think I was eight years old. I told my mother I want to play like you. You have magic hands."

"How old were you when you started?" she asks Madeline.

"I was nine," Madeline answers.

"Same age as me. Dexterity didn't come easy; my teacher gave me tons of finger exercises, and I hated them all," Martha tells her.

"No pain, no gain," Lynnwood adds.

"You sound like my teacher. She'd tell me to be patient and tough. Someday this pain will be useful to you," Martha tells them.

"It's impossible to imagine the usefulness when you're in the middle of claw hammers, windmills and arpeggios," Madeline replies.

"Magic hands produce magic sounds," Martha says to Madeline. "Magic sounds produce beautiful, magical expressions akin to decent food or the high some get from a drug. I love it when a musical piece evokes an emotion of nostalgia. Some pieces I perform remind me of happy moments from my childhood."

Madeline can remember as early as age five traveling with her parents. She remembers Christmas and Easter celebrations at church and the first time she attended summer camp. Madeline keeps her poise throughout the rest of their conversation, but the minute Lynnwood took Martha's hand and left the room, Madeline did a celebratory dance, jumping and eventually falling on the couch, astonished her childhood hero was in the audience watching the performance. She wishes her parents, particularly her mother, were present to see the great Martha Austin conversing with her daughter. When Madeline opens the door to leave the dressing room, Gregory Washington III is there holding a bouquet of nymph and rêvé amaryllis.

"We need to talk," he tells her.

"Where's Gracie?" Madeline looks over his shoulder.

"I'm here alone." He gives her the bouquet.

She reluctantly receives them. Their scent is sweet and heady. "Thanks. Why didn't you bring Gracie?"

"She had other plans," he tells Madeline.

With that information, Madeline figures he probably didn't tell her.

As they proceed down the hall and out into the atrium, Madeline notices theater staff still scrambling and moving like worker bees. The lights in the atrium have turned up bright. Madeline sees the night sky flash followed by a roll of thunder; its strong rumblings vibrate the structure. They sit.

"You just missed Martha Austin. She stopped by my dressing room."

"Who is that?" Gregory asks.

"You don't remember her?"

"Should I?" Gregory answers.

"Never mind. What did you want to talk about?" Madeline checks her watch to see the time.

"Kismet. Second chances. Signs," he answers.

Madeline holds up a hand. "I know where you're going with this."

"The other night after I saw you, I couldn't stop thinking about us," Gregory tells her.

"Gracie has so much talent. She left Juilliard for you."

"Whether or not she graduated from Juilliard, it wouldn't have made a difference," Gregory says.

"You told me something similar, and I'm so glad I didn't listen to you."

"You give the school too much credit."

"Anyway, Gregory, it's late, and I know my cousin Gracie is wondering where you are."

"Trust me, she's not worried. I left her in a château in Versailles sipping Dom Perignon in a garden tub surrounded by rose petals. See, that could've been you, but you wanted a baller with a bad-boy reputation. How is that working out for you?"

"We're four years in, and I couldn't be happier. I'm where I need to be—with who I need to be with." She gives the fragrant bouquet back to Gregory. At that moment, Lynnwood appears, walking through the atrium lobby, and his eyes meet Madeline's the minute she stands.

"Everything okay?" he asks. Walking over, he notices the bouquet in Gregory's lap.

"Everything is fine. I was getting ready to leave, and my old friend Gregory was waiting with me until my ride arrived."

Gregory stands and extends his hand. "Gregory Washington III."

"Lynnwood Tremé." Lynnwood shakes his hand. He glances at Madeline and the bouquet Gregory leaves sitting on the settee.

"Goodbye, Gregory," Madeline tells him.

When they embrace, his aroma and the memories of time spent with him fade quickly. After they pull apart, a look of longing appears in his eyes.

"Please give Gracie my love, and I'm happy for the two of you. Really I am," Madeline tells him.

"Mes bras sont toujours ouverts pour que tu retres à la maison," he tells her. Madeline doesn't have a clue that he is simply telling her his arms are always open for her to come home. Even the exquisite, lyrical sound of his French doesn't excite her the way it used to. Now it's cacophonous, and if she could talk to Gracie at that mo-

ment, she would tell her to run. She'd tell her no amount of luxurious creature comforts is enough to stand in the way of her purpose.

"Good night," she tells him.

"The cab's outside waiting for us," Lynnwood tells Madeline.

"Thank you," she tells Lynnwood.

He turns to Gregory. They shake hands. "Good evening. Be careful in the rain."

Lynnwood, with a guiding hand on the small of Madeline's back, opens a theater door to the sound of pouring rain. Lynnwood takes off his jacket, providing a cover for him and Madeline as they run and jump inside the backseat of a waiting cab.

They are drenched. The quick run from the theater to the cab in the downpour has them giddy with excitement. The Parisian lights and flashes of lightning give Madeline a clear view of Lynnwood. He takes off his glasses to wipe the lenses with a handkerchief. He examines the view through the lenses before placing them on his face.

"I was talking to Martha—she loved the show, saying you are the consummate performer. I said Madeline learned everything from her brother," Lynnwood says.

"I finally met Martha Austin. I can't wait to call Gilda and tell her about it."

"Where is she?" he asks.

"Had to fly back to Houston for some reason or another. She'll be back."

"Do you like her as your manager?"

"I trust Gilda more than anything and anybody."

"She should've been here tonight," Lynnwood says. "It's not often a big name like Martha Austin takes time out of their schedule to watch their contemporaries. When that happens, you seize that opportunity to build upon a working relationship. See, how you have staying power in this industry is networking with the right people."

"Our paths will cross again," Madeline says. "Word travels fast, you know better than anyone. We just keep being good. The rest will fall into place."

"Naïve of you to think it's that simple." Lynnwood runs a hand across his mustache as he looks out his window at French cafes and baroque turn-of-the-century facades.

They sit quietly for a moment as the sound of raindrops pounds on the roof. The windshield wipers work rapidly to clear the view for the driver.

"Thanks for coming back to check on me," Madeline says.

"Gregory Washington III." He chuckles. "Brother was cleaner than the board of health. He spoke French, had a beautiful bouquet of flowers...What happened to them?"

Madeline chuckles and shakes her head.

"I speak a little French. Homeboy says when you're ready, he's waiting with open arms."

Madeline looks at Lynnwood. "Stop. You know he didn't say that."

"I lived outside of Paris in a French village for a little over a year. I met this femme while on tour, and we shacked up. She spoke only French, and I picked up on a few words."

"You sure that's what you heard?"

"Loud and clear."

"I would never. I'm happily married. What's crazy, yesterday I discovered he's seeing my cousin."

"Where was she tonight?"

"He left her, thinking he could sweet talk his way back to me."

"Sounds to me like he had unfinished business."

"Whatever" is Madeline's response.

"You weren't having it."

"Hell no." Madeline is emphatic.

Lynnwood chuckles. "He had flowers, probably had a nice suite set up for you if you said yes."

"I don't care," Madeline responds.

"Was he that bad?"

"I'm not a fan of anyone who tries to control me."

"I agree." The tone of Lynnwood's voice turns serious. "What do you ultimately want, Maddie?"

"I want this—to work with the best and perform music that makes people laugh, cry, be nostalgic, motivate and inspire. I remember my mother always saying, 'Leave the world a better place than how you found it.' Our contribution, whether it's our original compositions or Ravel or Bach, makes the world better with the sound of music." Madeline stops. "I'm sounding like an infomercial."

"You said it," he replies.

Their cab pulls into the hotel's entrance. Lynnwood covers the fair. The wetness, the rain and night air causes Madeline's teeth to chatter. Once inside the elevator, Lynnwood pushes a button, and the door closes. The elevator opens to their floor. She opens her clutch to retrieve her key.

"Word to the wise..." Lynnwood begins. "Never allow your wants to supersede your needs." He walks ahead and opens the door to his suite on the other side of the hallway.

Madeline opens the door to her suite, and the moment it closes, she suddenly feels a desire to be held. She sheds her damp clothes and shoes and jumps into the shower, replaying the scene with Gregory and Lynnwood in her head. The more she thinks of Gregory, the angrier she gets. Once out of the shower, she dries off and dons the hotel's plush robe. She notices the answering machine blinking next to the phone. She presses the button to listen: "I just wanted to hear your voice. I love you."

It's JB. He's fifty-six hundred miles away, but the tone and texture of his voice never felt closer. Her tired and exhausted feelings of earlier are suddenly gone. JB is like an awakening—as he's been for the past five years—an awakener of all her curiosities and feelings. She opens the safe in her room where she keeps her notebook of compositions and her latest journal. Since her mother's death, she's kept a journal, complete with her thoughts, wishes and the day's activities. She grabs her journal.

Wednesday, July 1, 1992, 2:12 a.m.

I should be packing for the flight to Rome, but here I am, reflecting on life up to now. I'm twenty-two years old, married four years to a man who couldn't be more opposite, yet we've discovered our commonalities are aligned and when we're together we are harmonious. I am grapes growing on a vine; he's the vintner, crushing them to make delicious wine. He hears the notes. He says they come sometimes in his sleep; I am the composer who encapsulates his thoughts to write down on my sheet.

I miss him now. I'm thinking about Lynnwood's words: Don't let your wants supersede your needs. What do I want? I want to perform my music in concert halls all over the world. Why do I perform? There's nothing like being on stage with the spotlight and listening to chords and melodies and structures formulated to a sonata, or a suite, or a movement. The power of music knows no particular race or respect of person or class. The London and Paris elite enjoy watching me perform my "Sunset Composition" just as much as the little children I play for in the schools back in Harlem. What else do I want? I want doors to open for others who look like me, who enjoy listening to and performing two-hundred-year-old music.

Lynnwood says European audiences are more receptive, that's why when he was presented with the opportunity years ago, he accepted and wanted to bring along his finest musicians and a featured performer. At the time, he didn't know who he wanted to feature, but as time went on, it became clear. I appreciate Lynnwood. Usually someone of his considerable stature has an inflated ego, but so far, in the year and a half that I have known him, he's been level-headed and unassuming—almost too good to be true. Talk to the other musicians in the orchestra. They have a saying, "Must be good if you're playing with Lynnwood." He's won several Grammy awards and a Pulitzer for a musical composition. He told me he didn't need awards to validate his artistry reminded me of Gregory telling me I didn't need my degree from Juilliard. Speaking of which, I am furious—Gregory for the arrogant asshole he is, Gracie talented but foolish. I'm still disappointed—what a fool! Yes, I've gotten off track, but I was wise enough to immediately get right back on.

What do I need? Right now, I need to hear the sweet voice of my child. My dear, precious Melody. I am grateful for the village that is your Lola and Lolo, your grandmother and grandfather. When this tour is over, I promise to give you all the time and attention that you deserve. Little girls need the love of their mothers, I can't even begin to explain the bond my mother and I shared.

I need my husband. If he were here, he'd be writing down the lyrics to a song. I would be sitting nearby listening to him sing the melody before I input the notes on my staff sheet. We always remind each other that we are a team—each other's right hand. I need my husband here to hold and comfort me on this rainy night. I love it when he looks at me with yearning in his eyes. He can't get enough, and come to think of it, neither can I.

A sharp knock on the door startles her, jarring her thoughts. Her heart races to the point she hears it pounding. If she looks through the peephole, who will she see standing there? If it's who she thinks it is, what does he want? What does he need?

Sixteen

"No, Pops," JB tells his father, James.

James is taken aback.

"I gave you fifty-two for the property on Gulf Shores, seventy-five for the property on Panama Beach. A month ago, I wired you forty-five for the property near Tuskegee. I have family I've never met writing to my agent asking for money. Who gave them Levy's office address?"

"Son, when I was in the league, I gave back, and it didn't break the bank. You earn ten times more than I did, yet you can't write a ten-thousand-dollar check to your uncle?"

"Apparently, you haven't been made aware, but a tenth of my earnings were spent on your properties and monies given to relatives. I'm not Wells Fargo," JB says before walking down the hallway toward his parents' bedroom. He lightly taps on the door before his mother, Judy, answers. He opens the door to see his mother brushing Melody's hair.

"She's still coming with me?" he asks.

"Maybe later. I don't want her distracting you from working with the other children."

With that, JB walks outside and revs up the engine to his new Porsche. Seeing the shining candy apple red vehicle parked in the driveway must've prompted his father to ask him for more money. Though it was an impulse buy, what JB did with his money was his business. Four years ago, when he entered the league, he surprised his parents with vehicles—a new Porsche 911 Carrera in black for James and an alpine white BMW 750IL for Judy. He appreciates all the sacrifices they've made on his behalf, but he needs them to know, although he is a giver, he has limits. Once before, he told his father no. He suspects he will tell him no once again.

When JB arrives at the basketball camp, there are about sixty boys aged ten to seventeen, some with their parents, waiting. The neighborhood around them is slowly rebuilding. It's been two months since the riot. They call out his name, and he shows them basketball drills and gives them tips on improvement. He later gathers them for a pep talk. JB strides to the center of the court, the eager faces of young players watching him. His NBA jersey—more than a fabric—represents years of sweat, sacrifice, and resilience. The sun casts long shadows, and the air smells of freshly polished sneakers and youthful ambition.

"Look around," JB begins. "This court is where dreams ignite." He points to the hoop. "See that rim? It's not just metal. It's a gateway to possibility. Your dreams? They're the ball. Dreams alone won't cut it, you need hours in the gym, blisters on your fingers. The grind—it's where champions are made. Your alarm clock? It's your first opponent. Beat it." JB's gaze sweeps the crowd. "Basketball isn't solo. It's passes, screens and rebounds. Your teammates? They're your brothers. Celebrate their wins, lift them after losses. A team that fights together wins together. Fear?" JB leans in. "It's a liar. It'll tell you that you're too short or too slow." JB's eyes lock with a twelve-year-old. "Mindset matters. When you step on this court, you're not just playing basketball. You're rewriting your story. Believe you belong here. Visualize that game- winning shot. Feel the net swish."

As he walks and talks, he looks at the faces of the boys who listen, wide-eyed. When they entered the camp, they were given jerseys and new sneakers, courtesy of corporate donors who Anna convinced they needed to support a worthwhile cause.

"Friends might party," JB says, "but you're in the gym. Sacrifice. It's the price of greatness. Remember, you can't soar with anchors tied to your sneakers." JB's voice softens. "Someday you'll leave this court. But your legacy? It stays. Be more than stats. Be the kid who encouraged a teammate. Character matters. And when you make it?" He grins. "Pass the torch. Teach the next generation. Remember this court—it's where legends begin."

It's an hour and a half into the camp before Judy arrives with Melody. She sees a crowd gathered around JB as he signs his autograph on their basketballs. The sight of Judy and Melody catches his eye, and he signs a couple more basketballs before he takes Melody's small hand and guides her on how to dribble a basketball.

"See this?" he says, demonstrating a bounce. "That's dribbling. Keep it low, close to the ground." Melody mimics him, her eyes wide. The ball wobbles, but she persists. JB's heart swells. He remembers his father doing that for him. Each time she loses it, JB is there to guide it back to her hands. He then takes her to a basketball goal.

"Watch, Daddy." He stands midway between the goal and the free-throw line. He dribbles the ball before shooting it. The ball enters the net, hits the ground, and bounces back to him.

"I want to do it! Let me do it," Melody says.

JB gives her the ball. She tries to dribble it, her little tongue peeking out in concentration. She throws. The ball only reaches the bottom of the net.

"We'll keep trying," he tells her.

They attempt more times before he finally lifts her high enough to reach the net, and she throws the ball inside.

"That's Daddy's girl." He kisses and hugs her. "You're my MVP." He puts her down, and she runs to Judy's arms, and they watch JB teach more drills to the boys. Near the closing of camp, he's signing more basketballs and t-shirts and posing for pictures. His pager buzzes, and he recognizes Lilly's number. It's the number to her California address.

"Hey, Mom, I'll take Melody. Why don't you go shopping and treat yourself to something nice?" he tells her on the way to the car.

She glances at him rather strangely. Her eyes widen when he gives her his American Express.

"What's my limit?" she asks.

"Within reason," he tells her.

"Where are you and Melody going?"

"I don't know—Magic Mountain, Disneyland."

"And you don't need me? I mean you're not bothered by all the attention you'll get? You won't get a moment's peace," she tells him.

"When was the last time you had alone time?" JB asks.

Judy's eyes light up, and an overwhelming mixture of surprise showers her face.

"Pamper yourself. I got this," JB tells her as he opens her car door.

"Melody will be ready to eat soon. Don't give her any of that junk food at Magic Mountain or wherever you're taking her. When it's time for her to potty, make sure you go into the restroom stall with her. Had I known you were doing this, I would've brought extra clothing and packed her snacks."

"Moms, chill." JB chuckles.

"Give your Lola a kiss," Judy tells her. Melody gives her a hug and a kiss. "What time are you coming home?" Judy asks JB.

"You're giving me a curfew?" JB shakes his head.

Judy rolls her eyes. "Take care of my baby." She reaches into the backseat to give JB Melody's booster seat.

"*Your* baby?" JB takes it and closes the door. Judy waves goodbye before driving off.

JB places Melody in her booster seat and sits her in the backseat. Because space is compact in the sports car, he adjusts the passenger's seat so she can have more leg room.

"Let's ride," he tells her as he lets down the top.

***

JB and Lilly embrace when she opens the door. "My, aren't you a sight for sore eyes?" she says, kneeling to greet Melody. "Come." She pulls JB inside.

Her home smells of pine and grapefruit. Her daughter sits at a small table playing with an Etch A Sketch. Lilly introduces Melody to her three-year-old daughter whose name is Chloe. Their eyes are curious, and before long, they are playing and talking.

"Chloe, why don't you and Melody take the toys and play in the next room?" Lilly suggests.

Chloe takes her Etch A Sketch, and Melody follows her to another room.

JB finds a seat on the sofa. Lilly's style is organic. The ambiance and décor is earthy and soothing. On the wall hangs a giant family photo of Lilly, her arms are wrapped around Benny as he holds a four-month-old plumpy Chloe. Lilly's dressed comfortably in a white maxi dress and neutral-colored crisscross Birkenstock sandals. She sports her natural hair of course curls and not the knee-length faux goddess locs that smell of coconut. Lilly is that girl with bushy eyebrows, naturally kissable, succulent lips, and hair everywhere.

JB was a student at 'SC when he first laid eyes on her naked body. He noted her hairiness—body and armpits—and how she was comfortable and secure in her own skin. JB and millions of others, particularly guys who watched her on network television, were drawn to her mesmerizing eyes; her soft, sweet voice; and free-spirited nature.

"Today, I officially filed for divorce," Lilly tells him.

"You okay?" he asks.

"I'm fine. It's Chloe I'm worried about. The cycle of divorce continues. My parents divorced. Benny's parents divorced. Chloe's growing up where it's meetings in a McDonald's parking lot and seeing her father every other weekend. She's a trooper."

"You deserve better."

"When this is finished, my priorities are Chloe and my career, *if* I ever get it back on track."

"If?"

"I was never forgiven for the career decisions I've made."

"Forgiven by whom?"

"My ex-castmate."

JB thinks about Anna's sister, Mona, and the story Anna shared with him regarding the same castmate.

"Don't sweat it. I wouldn't."

"Easy for you to say."

"Shifting gears..." JB gathers his thoughts. "Remember when you were in the thick of it and how we used to go on our walks?"

"It feels like you're about to drop a bombshell."

"Someone was following us, snapping photos."

Lilly frowns. "How do you know?"

"A manila folder was left at the door of our apartment. Naturally, Maddie and I were curious. She opened it, and there were photos of you and me."

Lilly gasps, covering her mouth.

"Imagine the difficulty of explaining them to Maddie. I told her all we did was talk, which you and I know. Still, she wasn't convinced."

"I'm sorry." Lilly's soft tone expresses deep remorse.

"Things are still kind of murky for us," JB tells her.

"I've got an idea. I'll call and explain to her."

"No. Trust me. I've done enough," JB replies.

"Dealing with Benny and his infidelities, all I could think about was not feeling hurt and betrayed. You listened and literally held my hand. I'm sorry if it's caused tension with you and your wife."

"We need to stop paging and calling each other," JB tells her.

"I understand."

"I decided I wanted to tell you this in person."

"Your wife is a lucky woman. She doesn't have to worry. You're a keeper, unlike Benny." She sighs.

"Don't think for once I didn't have thoughts," JB tells her.

"I value our friendship. I'm glad we both chose not to take it there this time," she says. Silence follows as they take into consideration what Lilly just said. "Anyway, I...*ummm*...I have a friend who has a farm in Topanga. She has Shetland ponies, baby llamas and cute, furry baby chicks. The girls would love it," Lilly says, shifting the tone.

"Let's go," he tells her.

They gather their daughters and walk out the door.

"I like your car," Lilly says, walking around admiring it, "but it's too small." Lilly opens her garage. Inside is a white 1965 Ford Mustang and a red Jeep Cherokee.

"Take your pick," she tells him.

"Jeep for the win," he replies.

Just as Lilly assists the girls getting in the backseat and fastened into their booster seats, Benny rolls up in the driveway on his motorcycle, revving the motor. He hops off wearing denim jeans, steel-toe boots and a white t-shirt and leather vest. His locs are pulled back, and he's sporting Ray-Ban aviator shades.

"What the hell is going on?" he asks, glaring at JB and Lilly.

"Why are you here?" Lilly asks.

"To see my daughter and discuss the divorce papers," he answers.

"Everything is self-explanatory. I have nothing to say to you," Lilly tells him. "Now, leave. We've got somewhere to go, and you're holding us up."

"What a minute. Nobody's going anywhere," Benny says.

"Don't try and act like a husband and father now." Lilly's usually soft tone is now harsh.

"Look, I don't want any problems. I'm here as a friend," JB tells him.

"Friend? Same friend who hangs out with me in the studio? The same friend who bones my wife?" Benny calmly walks closer to JB.

"I don't know if you knew it or not, but I've got a wife, too. Not that it matters to you, but I need to put this out there. I value my wife, and I value my friendship with Lilly. If Lilly tells me she's hurting and you're the reason she's hurting, to me, it only makes sense to help her find a solution."

"Best thing you can do is stay out of our business." Benny walks closer.

Lilly stands between them. "Come on, Benny. Don't do this. Chloe and I haven't seen you since your tour ended, and that was months ago. You've got in your twisted head that JB and I are doing something because you're guilty."

Benny moves Lilly aside.

"Benny, stop." She places herself between him and JB again. "Please go."

Benny moves her aside and inches closer to JB. "You're a two-faced, backstabbing son of a bitch."

At five-foot-nine, he strikes six-foot-eight JB with a right-hand uppercut to the chin. JB loses his footing and stumbles against the motorcycle. The muffler, still hot, burns the back of his leg, causing him to emit a yell so ferociously loud, the neighbors hear it. Now the girls are screaming and crying from inside the Jeep. Lilly runs to them, closing the garage door behind her. When Benny charges at JB, his mouth connects with the sharp, bony part of JB's elbow. Benny grabs his face in pain. JB, still in pain, manages to grip Benny in a headlock. Every muscle and vein in his arms are visible as he constricts Benny. His face is red from straining. A black-and-purple bruise from Benny's uppercut is visibly etched on his face. Benny struggles, gasping for his next breath.

The urge to snap Benny's neck consumes JB's thoughts. He deserves it for all his indiscretions. He's seen him more than once while working alongside him in the studio engage in relations with groupies and sometimes other female artists. Lilly told him stories of finding lingerie in Benny's glove compartment. JB would never tell her what he witnessed. Benny's actions sent her emotions in a whirlwind. The night Lilly cried herself to sleep in his arms, he fought the extreme urges within him, remembering what he read from the verse his father-in-law, Eugene, gave him regarding love.

Within minutes, police sirens and flashing lights are upon the scene. JB finally releases his hold on Benny who coughs and pants, still gasping for air. His half-Black, half-Jewish yellow complexion is the color of a vibrant red inferno. JB's face is swollen, and an electrifying pain pulsates from the burn. Two white police officers jump out of their vehicles with guns drawn.

"Hands up," one of them shouts.

JB complies. Benny is still coughing and struggling to breathe.

"Face down on the pavement," an officer barks at JB, his Sig Sauer p320 is still drawn.

JB complies. Every nerve inside him struggles as he feels the cold, steel handcuffs clasp tightly against his wrists. In that moment, he thinks about Melody, but more so, how in the hell is he going to explain this to Madeline?

Seventeen

Basha stops mid dress when she glances at the television to see an Entertainment Tonight segment with JB, Lilly, and Benny. The headline reads, "Love Triangle Explodes."

On the screen, she sees a house and hears a voice-over recording: "Nine-one-one. What's your emergency?" A female dispatcher's voice is heard.

Another female who sounds white and older responds, "Yes, there are two Black men fighting. We need the police right away."

The next image is a mugshot of JB. His face is bruised and swollen. Staring into the camera, his eyes are cold and piercing. The sight grips Basha, holding her captive. Images of JB slam dunking and finishing with a face of triumph. Benny on a concert stage in dark shades strumming a Gibson Flying V. Lilly, in an old episode of *The Show,* with the reporter saying, "If charged, he could face up to six months in jail. If you remember, this is not the NBA star's first brush with the law. In 1987, he faced accusations of statutory rape."

Immediately, Basha thinks of an idea.

***

Basha knocks on the door, and within minutes, it opens. She follows the agent into a room with no windows, just a fluorescent light, a desk, two chairs and a filing cabinet.

She opens her portfolio to show the agent the photos.

"You took these?" he asks.

"Yes."

He scrutinizes every detail in the photos. "Fifteen hundred is my offer."

It was the third photo syndication agency on her list, and so far, his offer was the highest one yet. She retrieves them to place into her portfolio.

"You do nice work," he tells her.

"I know," Basha replies.

"Two grand. Final offer."

"I sell for two grand; you print the magazines with the photos, and they fly off the racks. How can I earn a percentage from each sale?"

"You freelance. My advice: Take a hundred more of these before you talk about percentages. In the meantime, two grand. I'll write a check."

"I prefer cash."

"Got chutzpah walking around this city with cash."

"Do you want these or not?" Basha snaps.

He pays her in one-hundred-dollar bills. Basha's next stop is back to Mona's apartment where she stuffs all her clothing into her suitcase. She remembers her toiletries and some articles of clothing in the bathroom. She must go through Mona's bedroom to retrieve them. She tries to open the door, but it's locked. She knocks.

"Mona. Mona, are you in there?" She continues to knock, but there's no answer. She looks around the tiny apartment for things to take with her. None of the paintings can fit into her suitcase. The Swarovski and Baccarat figurines and picture frames can get her something if she pawns them. With the cash, she can buy new stuff. First, a one-way ticket back home to L.A.

***

Madeline is in Rome. The shows for all three nights are sold out. Madeline and Lynnwood and members of the orchestra along with an Italian interpreter spend the morning doing press for Italian television. It's three in the afternoon when Gilda arrives at Madeline's hotel room. Her mood is somber.

"JB's been arrested," she tells Madeline.

"Arrested? Arrested for what?"

"Assault."

"Who did he assault?"

"Benny Manheim, the rock star."

Suddenly the images from the photos of JB and Lilly come to mind.

"Why?" Madeline asks, feeling her heart racing.

"Maddie, honey, that's something you'll need to inquire about when you talk to JB."

Madeline picks up the phone to page him, entering her code and phone number. She sits quietly at a desk anticipating it to ring any second.

"We have a soundcheck in the next hour or so," Gilda reminds her.

This time Madeline dials Judy's number. It rings continuously. Still, no answer. She drops it on the cradle.

"I will be okay. I will be okay. We'll go to soundcheck. I'll come back here, take a nap, and get ready for tonight's show," Madeline says as if she's thinking aloud to herself as opposed to telling Gilda, who sits nearby.

Gilda got news of JB's arrest from Judy hours before she was scheduled to board the flight to Rome. She hesitated whether to tell Madeline before or after the performance.

Madeline pages JB again and waits. Minutes pass. "I don't think JB is being up front with me about him and Lilly."

Gilda clears her throat. "As your manager, my job is to make sure you go on that stage tonight, and that your sound, look, and performance are clear and on point. As your mother figure someone who's known you since the day you were born, there are no right answers. Just know there are risks and there are rewards. No one knows the intricacies of you and JB's relationship better than you and JB. As I told you before, the distance between you is strenuous enough. Don't let communication suffer. Ask yourself: Is my marriage worth fighting for?"

"Why isn't he calling?" Madeline picks up the phone to page him again.

"Stop," Gilda tells her. "Trust he's gotten that page as well as the previous two."

Madeline looks at the time. "Watch, he'll call when I'm out."

"If that's the case, he'll leave a message. You'll see."

"Gilda."

"Yes?"

"Do you wonder about Daddy sometimes? Do you believe him when he tells you he's out golfing or at a conference or counseling some member at the church?"

"Maddie, life is about choices. I knew once I chose to marry your daddy, I chose everything that came with marrying him, his full-time ministry—twenty-four/seven, 365 days of it. I knew the rewards, and I knew the risks. I knew that I couldn't have him all to myself, and I was okay with it. I also knew that beside every great man is a woman whose role is greater. I knew it wasn't easy, but that's the covenant I chose to make with God and your daddy."

"What you're saying is I knew what I signed up for the minute I chose to get with JB. Oh boy, you live and learn." Madeline sighs.

"What's the lesson you've learned from this?"

"When life gets messy, take the lessons and put the message in a song. It's the only way I know how to deal with it."

Gilda nods. "Life can be a song. One minute, it's Felix Mendelsohn's 'Wedding March,' years later it's B.B. King's 'The Thrill is Gone,' or it could be 'Solid,' like Ashford and Simpson."

"Aunt Mary told me when you're involved with a pilot, a pro athlete, even a pastor...there's bound to be pain. But she said for me to have peace, I've got to pray. I don't pray enough."

"God hears you."

"He does?"

"Of course He does," Gilda answers.

"I've always wondered, if that was the case, why didn't He hear me when I was praying for Mother?"

"Did you ever stop to consider God knows the bigger picture?"

"No," Madeline answers.

"That's why I never question. I believe there is a purpose for everything, even things we don't consider fair or just."

Madeline looks at her watch and the telephone on the desk. "I guess he's not calling."

"He will."

"You don't understand. JB and I have not spoken to each other in weeks." Madeline buries her face in her hands out of frustration. "Who goes that long without picking up the phone?"

Gilda looks at her watch. "How about we skip the soundcheck?"

"No, let's go," Madeline tells her.

Gilda studies Madeline who walks into the bathroom to make a last check at her appearance. She washes her face, dries her tears, applies more makeup, and goes on as usual.

When Madeline meets up with Lynnwood and the rest of the orchestra for a soundcheck, she can't help but wonder if it was indeed Lynnwood knocking on her door the other night. She sat in bed paralyzed as she heard the door knock about four times. The rain and thunder intensified, and the lightning produced a show and the words *Love does not dishonor* echoed like a mantra consuming her thoughts. For as long as she's known Lynnwood, she's never looked at him in any way but professionally, but in the car on the ride to the hotel, she sensed something she couldn't quite put her finger on.

* * *

Applause and cheers of bravo ring throughout the auditorium. The love and appreciation from the audience touch Madeline in a way she never felt from previous performances in London and Paris. After the show, she and Lynnwood do their usual meet and greet, which lasts until early morning. Concert goers can't get enough of them. Madeline, Gilda, Lynnwood, and a handful of orchestra members catch a taxi to a nightclub. There, they party until daybreak. Madeline returns to her hotel room to see a message light blinking on the phone. She presses it, placing it on the speaker. Exhausted, she takes off her heels and collapses on the bed.

"Maddie." It's JB's voice. "I really wish you'd pick up sometimes."

She pages him and puts in her room number and a code to let him know it's her. She's deep in a coma like sleep when the telephone rings. She blindly reaches for it before finally picking it up.

"Hello," she answers.

"Hey. What's up?"

"Why haven't you called?"

"I have. You just haven't been answering. How is the tour?" he asks.

"It's going great. The Rome shows have sold out."

"That's good."

"I understand why Americans tour Europe. They appreciate our music."

"That's good" is JB's reply.

There is an awkward moment of silence.

"Something I need to tell you," JB begins.

Although Madeline already knows, her ears ring, and her heart still races.

"I got arrested a couple of days ago. Benny and I got into a fight because he thinks I was sleeping with Lilly."

"Where did this happen?"

JB sighs. "At Lilly's place."

"Why were you there?"

"I wanted to tell her about the photos."

"Why was it so important for you to do it in person?"

"That's the part I struggle with. Why did I even need to tell her about them, period? This nonsense could've been avoided. Now the media's taken it and turned the narrative into a love triangle."

"A love triangle?"

"Yes."

"Tell me what happened."

"Benny pulled up on his motorcycle, just as I was leaving Lilly's house. One word led to another, and he...punched me in the face. I fell on his motorcycle and burned the back of my leg on the motorcycle pipe. He was coming after me, so I blocked another punch with my elbow, but it happened so fast the bone in my elbow cut his lip, and it must've caught him off guard. In that split second, I lunged and put him into a chokehold I swear, something came over me because I was about to snap his neck. The police showed up and saw me with Benny in a chokehold. Meanwhile Benny's gasping for air. Police arrested me and took me to jail. Meanwhile, every station in L.A. is talking about it. I was supposed to have a press conference to announce my decision to play with Chicago, but now it's uncertain."

"You're leaving New Jersey?"

"Yes."

"Why didn't *we* have this discussion?"

"Like *we* didn't discuss you taking a five-month tour of Europe?" JB reminds her.

"How dare you make this about me, JB."

"Sorry," he says, and after minutes of silence, "I miss you."

Madeline is seething. "First, I walk in on you having phone sex with her. Next, I see photos of you holding her hand and kissing her forehead. Now, you've gotten arrested for assaulting her husband...JB, do you think I'm stupid?"

"I know the shit looks suspect, but I swear on my Grandma Imogene, all we did was talk...and hold hands. That's it."

"And that's too much considering you're a married man, JB."

"Maddie, trust and believe this: Every part of you fulfills every inch of me. Why do you think I can't keep my hands off you? When we're together, we make love three, sometimes four and five times a day. You fill me up. You."

"Just words with absolutely no meaning, JB."

There is silence on the other end.

"Hello," Madeline begins. "You tell me in words nothing's happening, but your actions dictate otherwise."

"I need you right here next to me."

"Stop."

"I'm not playing games. I need you."

"Tell that to the people here in Rome, and Helsinki, and Stockholm, and Geneva, and Berlin, and Copenhagen, and Brussels."

"Fuck it. I see what your priorities are."

"I'm under contract. I just can't leave. You think I can ask you to stop playing ball in the middle of a game?"

"This is not about basketball or music; this is about you and me. I'm in a crisis, and I need my wife. Is that too much to ask?"

The intensity of Madeline's pounding heart causes her entire body to shiver. Lying there in a plush early twentieth century bed, her mind races. A decision must be made with expediency and urgency.

Eighteen

JB pulls into the private entrance of the hotel and valets his Porsche with the attendant. Upstairs, seven stories up in a suite, sits his father-in-law who caught a flight out as soon as he could. Newspapers and tabloid magazines still report on the supposed love triangle. It's been four days since the story broke, now the pictures of JB with Lilly have surfaced.

JB braces himself for what's to come. He greets Eugene with a firm fatherly hug.

"Poppa E," JB calls him.

"You're still my favorite son-in-law," Eugene responds.

"That's good to know. Maddie might not think too fondly of me these days."

"Exactly what I want to talk about."

JB feels his palms sweating as he rubs his thighs, wearing athletic track pants.

"I got this in the mail." Eugene drops the manila envelope in JB's lap.

JB is hesitant. It looks like the envelope he and Madeline saw sitting outside their door. Only this envelope contains a postmark from New York, New York, and the postmark was dated in May.

"Go ahead. Open," Eugene tells him.

"What's in it?" JB's eyes are suspicious.

"Open it," Eugene insists.

JB opens it and sees the photos of himself with Lilly along with the photos of Madeline with Lynnwood.

"What's the story here?" Eugene asks.

"How did you get this?" JB responds.

"It was mailed to the church."

JB's mind races. Madeline told him they got lost during the move. Did she lie and mail them to her father instead?

"It was sitting in the stack of mail along with my devotionals. I opened it, and my heart dropped when I saw you and another woman. I said, '*That's not Madeline.*' I looked further and saw photos of Madeline with Lynnwood, and I said, 'That's not JB.'"

JB clasps his hands and leans forward to gather his thoughts.

"Someone at the church saw your story on television and informed me of your arrest. I said, 'You're sadly mistaken. My son-in-law is much too cool to blow his top.'"

"It's crazy, Poppa E."

Eugene sits in a chair across from JB with his legs crossed. "I'm not on a schedule. In fact, I've cleared my calendar for the next two days."

JB rocks quickly back and forth. "I love Madeline with everything in me," he begins. "She gives me all I need. Now, I also have a friend who happens to be female. Backstory: We were once intimate—this was before I got with Madeline. She lived and worked on the East Coast; I was still attending 'SC. It didn't work out for us, yet we remained friends. She moved on, met Benny, he and I became friends—in fact, he's the one who introduced me to the production side of music. I've watched him write, play several instruments, record, and mix them and make it sound like several musicians performing. Musically, the brother is a genius. Some nights, when Maddie was at Juilliard, busy doing her thing, I'd hang out with him in the same studio where Jimi Hendrix once recorded. Just like he was a master at the control boards and the music, he was also fond of the ladies—mind you, he and Lilly were now married with a baby."

"Weren't you also in the studio with him when these ladies were around?"

JB chuckles. "Poppa E, I see where you are going. No lie, beautiful women came through, and I admit I've flirted with quite a few of them, but I draw the line when it comes to infidelity. That's where Benny and I clashed. Sometimes Lilly would page him, and he never answered. Too busy getting busy."

"How did she find out about Benny?"

"The girls he fooled around with left clues—lingerie in the glove compartment, sometimes they'd call the house."

"How did you get involved?"

"One day Lilly stopped by the studio, and I happened to be there working on a song. She was looking for Benny who had just left. I was surprised they didn't run into each other. She stayed there thinking he was coming back, but he never did. That night, I remember walking her home and listening to her vent all her frustrations. From that moment on, I guess you could say I became her confidant."

"And where was Maddie during those times?"

"Juilliard became her third home."

"Was there ever a moment where instead of spending quality time with Maddie you instead spent time with Lilly?"

JB thinks about the question. "Not that I recall."

"I'm trying to understand, how do you go from friend in the studio to foe in the driveway?" Eugene sits, his eyes in study mode, his ears attuned. "You think someone sent him these photos? Think that could've prompted him?"

"Poppa E, I'm still trying to figure it out because someone sent those same photos to our apartment in New York."

"Maddie's seen these?"

"Yes."

JB leans forward, clasping his hands to his lips. He rocks quickly back and forth. His eyes flit.

"What's happening right now?" Eugene asks, studying JB.

"Like I mentioned before, it's crazy."

"How?"

"I can't explain it." JB's voice is barely above a whisper.

"How did you and Madeline get to this place?"

"We both want what we want, and we don't let anything stand in our way—even if the thing standing in the way is a spouse, a marriage, a child, family obligations."

"Can you honestly see a marriage continuing at this rate?" Eugene asks.

A minute passes before JB responds, "I don't know."

JB's pager vibrates constantly as they talk. He finally checks it, seeing Levy, Anna, Caleb, Judy, James, Caleb, and Paul's numbers.

"It's my agent," he tells Eugene.

"There's a phone in the other room," Eugene tells him.

JB excuses himself to call Levy. It rings several times before Levy answers.

"What up? What up?" JB wants to know.

"Chicago's holding off on the trade."

"Why?"

"Pending personnel needs."

"Does my situation have anything to do with it?"

"The organization is protecting its brand. I'm afraid your high-profile situation brings too much negative press."

"Bullshit. I know they're not over there acting like a fucking Boy Scout troop."

"These things happen all the time, and with some players, the issue gets swept under the rug. We'll wait until this simmers down."

"I can't afford to wait. Next, you'll be calling to tell me they scraped my national campaign and Gatorade is a miss."

"Not happening. Trust me."

"If Chicago has cold feet, I know a place where I won't need to worry about it ever getting cold."

"Where is that?"

"Houston. They could use me more than Chicago."

"They are a team to watch, but in the meantime, I'll need to make some more phone calls. I'll follow up with you tomorrow," Levy tells him.

JB hangs up with Levy and calls Anna. She picks up on the third ring. "How is my Big Bad Wolf?" she answers.

"I'll need a game plan."

"I'm the game changer."

JB chuckles. "You'll forever be my nigga."

"I'd rather you call me your ace."

"Ace? Sounds like something your Italian cousins would say. We're in Cali, your mother's Black, therefore, I call you my nigga."

"Anyway, nigga, get your ass over here," she tells him.

JB looks at the time and hangs up. The nagging pain from the motorcycle burn bothers him. After the arrest, it was hours before he got treatment for the burn and blistering. He wasn't a stranger to iron penetrating his skin. As an undergrad, he was wild and inebriated when his fraternity branded its symbol on his left arm. This time, the burn totally caught him off guard.

He walks in to see Eugene reading a magazine.

"Poppa E, I gotta go."

Eugene walks him to the door. "I'm here for a couple of days."

"I appreciate the talk." JB gives him a firm hug.

"Always remember, no weapon formed against you shall prosper. A weapon isn't always tangible—it can be words, thoughts, deeds." Eugene looks him in the eye.

"I'll remember that," JB says before the door closes behind him.

***

JB arrives at Anna's. It's late. She's wearing no makeup, in a USC sweatshirt and shorts. Hair from her classy bob is tucked behind her ears.

"What the hell happened to you?" she asks.

"I'm tired of explaining it. I'm starting to sound like a fucking broken record."

He walks to her wet bar, opens a bottle of tequila and pours himself a shot. "You need one?" he asks her.

"Why not?" She watches as he grabs another shot glass and pours.

"Where's the salt?" he asks.

"We don't need it," Anna tells him.

"My nigga," he says before raising his glass. "To those who wish me well, and all the rest can go to hell." He and Anna clink glasses before downing.

"Smooth," he says, nodding.

"Good tequila doesn't require salt. You act like I haven't taught you anything."

They have a seat on Anna's cream-colored velour sectional. Anna's home is modern and airy, with high ceilings, windows and 360-degree views of Los Angeles.

"Are you screwing Lilly again?" she asks.

"No."

Anna gives him a glance like she doesn't believe him. "With the exception of me and probably your wife, I've always questioned your taste in women."

"Lilly is sweet, simple, real, and comfortable in her skin. She isn't into high-end fashion, although she can very well afford it. She's organic and not superficial, it makes her endearing. Whereas Maddie loves rare pieces of the finest jewelry, Lilly prefers a first edition collection of poems by Nikki Giovanni."

"You're sexing her. Why else would you and Benny come to blows?"

"Benny's the one screwing around, so naturally he assumes we're doing the same."

"Why were you there?"

JB thinks about it. "I can't believe I'm saying this, but you'd understand or maybe not. I wanted to tell Lilly in person that we needed to stop paging and talking on the phone about her issues with Benny. I remember one night, Maddie walked in on us talking on the phone, and I was..."

"You were doing what?" Anna's eyes dance from his eyes to his lips.

"The five-knuckle shuffle."

She scoffs. "How did you explain that?"

"It doesn't even matter. I draw the line when it comes to infidelity. I was talking to my father-in-law tonight just before I got here, and he said weapons aren't always tangible—they can be words, thoughts, and deeds."

"You think your mind is a weapon?" Anna asks.

"I know it is," JB responds.

"I...um...do you remember Gadise from my party weeks back?" Anna asks.

"Yep." JB's eyes smile as his memory recalls sitting next to her.

"Why are you smiling?" Anna looks curious.

"It's nothing," he answers. "What about her?"

"She's interested in developing a sports documentary about you. Now, with all the news of you, Benny and Lilly and the previous issues with you and the nature of your relationship with your wife, it's an opportunity for people to see a different side of you—how you're a humanitarian, how you conduct basketball camps for inner-city kids, how you love to write and produce music in your spare time, how you love and cherish your wife and daughter. I want you to be relatable, loveable, and still be the star on an untouchable level."

"I'm cool with it except the part with Maddie and Melody. I want to keep them private."

"But your wife's a public figure too."

"Not to the extent that I am."

"I'll make note of it," Anna says.

"Thank you," JB says, nodding. He looks into her eyes. "You're always looking out for me."

"I gave you my word I would. Now leave and go to your wife."

"She's in Rome," he says.

"You and Maddie need to come together and work through this crisis like really soon, it's not a good look for you if she's long distance."

With that, Anna stands and extends her hand to him. He takes it and follows her. He hasn't had strong sexual desires for her in years, but it's been weeks since Madeline left for Europe, and now he has an ache that defies reason. Anna's hand, cool against his palm, guides him through the dimly lit hallway. He imagines her leading him upstairs, the soft rustle of fabric, the warmth of skin against skin. Instead, she leads him to the entryway where they stand. Their eyes lock—a silent conversation. Anna's lips part, but instead of whispered promises, she utters a command: "Go home."

The words cut through the charged atmosphere when she opens the door. JB nods and steps into the night.

Nineteen

Madeline constantly knocks on Gilda's hotel room door until it opens. She appears agitated with her face covered in a creamy green mask, wearing a silk hair bonnet and a carnation-colored terry-cloth robe.

"We need to talk," Maddie tells her.

Without a word, Gilda opens the door wide enough for Madeline to enter. Her room has a view of hundreds-years-old Roman architecture buildings.

"I just got off the phone with JB. He's begging me to come home."

Gilda sighs. "You can't do that. You have performances tonight and tomorrow."

"I think he's sabotaging me. JB never wanted me to tour, and now he's thinking of ways to get me to quit."

"After tonight's show, you have five days off before the next performance. Take the opportunity to fly back then. Right now—shows are selling out—not because of Lynnwood but because of you. Contractually, you have obligations for the next one hundred and thirty days."

"I get so tired of dealing with JB sometimes, Gilda. You just don't understand," Madeline cries.

Gilda nods and quietly crawls into bed and covers up. Madeline gets it's her cue to leave. She trudged down the corridor to her room, and when she stands in front of her door, she realizes she's left her key inside. She dreads walking to the lobby in her robe with green clay covering her face. She finds a courtesy phone located near the elevators to call downstairs and request a staffer bring up a new room key.

While she's waiting near the elevators, Lynnwood appears, dressed casually, sporting a hat, and carrying his shiny brass trumpet. Madeline freezes, her cheeks flushing a shade of mint to match her facial mask. Lynnwood's eyes widened, and he tried—and failed—to suppress a laugh.

"Well," he says, "I've heard of face masks, but this is a whole new level of camouflage."

Madeline gestures to her face. "It's my secret weapon," she mumbles. "Instant relaxation."

Lynnwood leans closer, examining the mask. "Is it made from crushed unicorn tears or something?"

"It's just mint and clay. But close—I left my key in the room," Madeline tells him. "I'm waiting here until someone from the hotel staff brings me another one." Her eyes, though tired behind the mask, manage to sparkle of their own volition as she does a brief study of his ensemble. "I'm surprised you're not asleep."

"Always had this desire to play my trumpet at St. Peter's Square and watch the pigeons scatter about."

Madeline smiles, displaying a row of pearly whites. "Why am I getting a visual?"

"I would invite you to come along, but—"

Their quiet moment is interrupted when the elevator opens and a hotel staffer appears. "I'm who you're looking for," she tells him. She turns to Lynnwood. "Enjoy the plaza with the pigeons. I really need to get some sleep. You wouldn't want me falling over the keys tonight."

"True. We can't have you playing with your forehead," he tells her.

Madeline grins, the green mask cracking. Then she remembers the last night in Paris. "Was it you?" she blurts out. "The one knocking on my door?"

Lynnwood's smile holds secrets—the kind that only Paris can keep. "Madeline," he says, "some stories are best left in the City of Light." He presses the button to the elevator. It opens immediately before he steps inside.

Madeline's heart skips a beat as the elevator doors slide shut.

Once she's inside her room, she's wide awake. She gathers her lotions and creams and pampers herself, making a mental note of the last time she's been able to do such. She undresses and looks at the curves of her naked body in the mirror. She sees her 40DD breasts have sagged since giving birth and seven months of nursing. There's a stubborn stomach pooch that only goes away when she sucks it in to put on a girdle. She buys pregnancy tests and birth control as often as she buys sanitary napkins. She looks at her container of pills, and she's up to date. No more surprises, though she doesn't remember if she missed a couple of days as the reason for the last pregnancy.

She wants to go out and see the city and maybe listen to Lynnwood's trumpet against the backdrop of age-old ruins and monuments. What did he mean when he said, "Some stories are best left in the City of Light?" She can't fall for Lynnwood, in no way, shape, form or fashion. Then she remembers JB, gets angry and tears fall. She eventually cries herself to sleep.

* * *

It's always in that moment when the spotlight shines upon her and the audience applauds that she instantly gets goosebumps. As with every performance, she waits until the room is completely silent before she plays the first note. When the melody comes together and the rest of the orchestra plays along, she is caught up in the magic and beauty of it all. This is the seventh performance, and there's something different that Madeline can't put her finger on. It's the idea her problems are thousands of miles away and can't in any way hinder her performance. She's radiant in a black sequined dress, wearing a diamond necklace and earrings that once belonged to her mother. Her eighteen inches of hair are pulled back into her signature chignon. Photographers capture a range of her emotions—the moments when she's smiling wide at the audience. Other moments where her eyes are closed and she's lost in the music, the diamonds in her necklace sparkling.

Rome showers them with love and treats them like rock stars. When Madeline and Gilda arrive back at the hotel, Gilda tells her she's in for the night and hangs the do not disturb sign before she closes the door. Madeline returns to her room to change out of her dress and shower. She lets down her hair, allowing it to fall past her shoulders.

Walking through the lobby, she recognizes musicians from the orchestra sitting at the bar. They spot her heading in their direction, sporting palazzo pants with a low-cut backless designer blouse. She joins them at the bar.

"We didn't know you could be our kind of people," one states.

"*Ha, ha.* Consider me your musical wildcard," she answers.

She notices musicians drinking wine, and some are having cocktails.

"You drink?" someone asks her.

"No," she answers, "but after a show like tonight's, I'll make an exception."

"Start off with an Aperol spritz," someone suggests.

"It's not heavy, is it?" she asks.

"It's prosecco. You'll like it," another musician suggests.

Bartenders mix and pour, and before long she's cheering, toasting, and laughing along with the rest. The name of a night club is mentioned, and six of them pile into a taxi. Madeline's sitting on a musician's lap—a cellist—and finds the sensation rather strange. Inside the nightclub, the air is thick. Flickering candle lights dance across the walls, casting shadows that seem to sway to an invisible rhythm. She hears a familiar riff and a phrasing that can be no other than Lynnwood. His presence commands attention—a blend of confidence and vulnerability. His trumpet, polished to a golden sheen, gleams under the spotlight. He's performing with other musicians from the orchestra she recognizes. She moves through the crowd, inching closer to the stage. Lynnwood blows, and the note hangs in the air like a delicate thread, weaving through the hearts of everyone present.

One thing Madeline notices about Europeans: They love American music. She heard Motown playing in the cab ride on the way to the nightclub. Last night, Bobby Womack's "Across 110th Street" played in the party mix. They spoke no English but knew every word to Tina Turner's "What's Love Got to Do with It."

Tonight, the Americans take over an Italian night club, but the locals don't seem to mind at all. As Lynnwood and the other musicians improvise, the room transforms. The ancient stone walls seem to sway, and the candle flames flicker in time with the rhythm. The audience leans forward, their eyes wide, as if afraid to miss a single nuance.

The nightclub ceases to exist—it is a portal to another realm, where music holds the power to ignite passion. Madeline's heart races. She feels the music wrap around her, pulling her closer to the stage. Lynnwood's eyes meet hers, and at that moment, they are the only two people in the room. His trumpet sings of love that transcends borders, cultures, and expectations. And then, as if surrendering to fate, Lynnwood plays the final notes. When he ends the musical set, the crowd yells in Italian. They want him to continue. He puts his trumpet back to his lips and plays. A double bass and drums accompany the slow tempo. His horn is slow, as if it is in mourning. He walks toward the edge of the stage and plays directly to her. When he's finished, he walks off the stage and through the crowd where he disappears. Madeline tries to enjoy the rest of the evening, but with Lynnwood gone, the atmosphere shifts.

She takes a cab, alone this time, to the hotel, and on her way to the room, she stops by Lynnwood's hotel room and knocks on his door. It opens, and he appears.

"Hey," he answers, his eyes curious.

"I like the song you performed at the club. You wrote it?"

"I did. It's a melody I've been hearing in my head since we started the tour."

"It's somber, like a stroll in the park at dusk."

"You want to come in?" he asks.

"No. I just want to say thanks for giving me this opportunity again. It's always been my dream."

"If I see true talent, I recognize it and bring it with me."

"And I am forever grateful," she says to him.

He nods, a smile touching his lips, an acknowledgment of her choice to keep the personal and professional as distinct as the notes on a scale. "Then, until our next concerto," he replies.

With a final glance, Madeline turns, her steps echoing down the hall, a counterpoint to the beat of her own heart. And as Lynnwood's door closes softly behind her, it's not an ending but a rest—a pause in their music that speaks of respect, of boundaries, and of the understanding that some harmonies are best left unwritten.

Twenty

Madeline is fast asleep as soon as the plane takes off from Rome. Last night's show followed up with an after party has her head reeling and her emotions swirling. She left it up to Gilda to inform Lynnwood of her sudden departure. Gilda agreed to stay behind to conduct matters for upcoming shows. Madeline immediately got on the phone to call JB to let him know she was coming. Madeline mentally prepares for what's in store once she lands. The very nature of handling her personal life while maintaining her professional image wears on her like a thick callus. She tosses and turns, finally awake hours before the plane schedules to land in Chicago. From there, she connects to another flight that departs for Los Angeles.

In the baggage area, just as she descends the escalator, the chauffeur Bo Young stands holding a sign with her name on it.

"Good evening. Welcome," he speaks.

She nods slightly, wondering why he's present and not her husband. A baggage handler retrieves her luggage pieces, placing them on a cart. He follows her and Bo outside where a black Lincoln Town Car awaits. Madeline is expecting to see JB waiting inside, instead there is a bouquet of roses in almost every color—from baby blue to lavender to yellow. Next to the bouquet is a small box and a handwritten note. Madeline recognizes JB's handwriting.

"May I close the door?" Bo asks.

"Where's JB?" she asks.

Bo smiles. "He gave me specific instructions."

"Oh? And what's that?" Madeline asks.

"He said be quiet and drive." Bo closes the door.

Madeline sits thinking, *What trick does JB have up his sleeve?* She unwraps the gift to find a box made of red velvet. She opens it, and there are rare pristine saltwater pearl earrings. The note accompanying it reads:

Maddie,

You are rare. Fine. Valuable. I could travel the world over and never find a more beautiful pearl.

As she's reading it, she hears his voice, a mellifluous baritone. Unlike his singing voice, which is tenor, his talking voice breaks down all her inhibitions—at least it did before. Looking out the car's window, she reads signs. They are traveling southbound on the 405.

"How's the temperature?" Bo asks.

"It's pleasant," she answers.

At times, the town car cuts through winds going nearly seventy miles per hour. Then there are areas of the expressway where the traffic comes to a crawl. The lull and jet lag put her to sleep. She awakens when the car stops. They are on the grounds of a Mediterranean stucco-style mansion.

Bo opens the door for her and carries all her bags inside.

"Thank you." She opens her pochette to retrieve dollar bills—a couple of twenties, a ten and several ones.

Bo politely refuses. "Have a wonderful evening," he says with a smile. The door closes, and it sounds like an echo in the large room. As Madeline steps into the grandeur of the Mediterranean mansion, her senses are immediately enveloped by the opulence that surrounds her. The foyer is a breathtaking expanse of terracotta tiles that gleam under the soft glow of an iron chandelier. To her left, an open-concept living space beckons, where natural woods and stone accents blend seamlessly with modern furnishings. The air carries the delicate fragrance of jasmine, mingling with the rich aroma of aged leather and polished wood.

As she ventures farther, the distant sound of a piano grows clearer, the notes flowing like water—soft and ambient, yet profound in their simplicity.

"JB," she calls out. She hears him playing Frédéric Chopin's "Prelude Op. 28 No 4." JB's playing is not just heard but felt, a peaceful melody that resonates with the very walls of the mansion. The music is like a gentle caress, a calm piano ambiance that fills the space with a sense of tranquility and upliftment. Madeline is drawn toward the music, each step bringing her closer to the source of the harmonious sound. She finds JB in a sunlit parlor, his silhouette framed against a backdrop of floor-to-ceiling windows that offer a view of the lush gardens outside. His fingers move with effortless grace over the keys, and she pauses to watch, the beauty of the moment not lost on her. She doesn't care that she's spent nearly seventeen hours on a plane or that her breath isn't the freshest. When the song ends, she wraps her arms around him.

"I'm here, baby," she whispers.

He takes her, and in one swift motion, lifts her into his arms, where he holds, kisses, and caresses her.

"Fly back to Europe with me," she tells him between kisses.

"Shhhhhh," he whispers, a gentle command in the quiet room. His eyes remain closed, savoring the moment as he holds her in his arms. The contrast is striking—the soft curves of her body pressed against the defined, athletic build of his body. It's a melding of strength and tenderness, a silent acknowledgment of their mutual need for this closeness. They linger in the embrace. When he finally opens his eyes, the world seems to pause, the intensity of his gaze locking with hers. In that prolonged look, a cascade of unspoken emotions passes between them—hope, fear, longing—all converging in a single, silent exchange that says more than words ever could.

"I'm here. Now what?" she asks.

He takes her hand and leads her to the bathroom. He turns on the faucet to the garden tub, adjusting the temperature before pouring the bubble bath. By the time he turns off the faucet, the tub is filled with bubbles. They undress and sit inside. The water is hot, but their bodies eventually adjust.

"There's talk Benny might consider filing charges." He says.

"You think he has a case?"

"I don't know."

"You didn't think about Melody and me and how it affects us?"

He's silent.

"JB, you don't understand how much this tour means to me. I don't want it to slip out of my hands. I've only got five days off, and I've already spent a day and a half of those flying."

He plants a slow, passionate kiss on her lips.

"We've got the next day or so together," he says. "You'll be everything to me—breakfast, lunch, dinner, dessert, my sleeping pill, my score keeper, my lover, the perfect love song with all the right lyrics."

Alone in the mansion, the vastness of space amplifies every sound and every breath. Her cries, a symphony of emotion, resonate through them, mingling with his moans, which speak of a passion unrestrained. These sounds of lovemaking—raw and unfiltered rise to the rafters, filling the expanse with the evidence of their love.

When their bodies aren't entwined, their souls meet in the realm of music. The mansion, with its echoing chambers and high ceilings, becomes their private conservatory. It's massive—a labyrinth of rooms and secrets and it's where they find a playground for their whimsy. JB and Madeline play a game of hide-and-seek, their laughter pealing like bells as they chase each other through the corridors. It's a game of shadows and light, of seeking and finding, a metaphor for the deeper search within their hearts. They are both lost and found, their cries and moans, their music and games, all echoes of the same profound truth that in the vastness of life, they have found a corner of the universe where they truly belong.

* * *

Anna pages JB. Her heart races. Her sister, Mona, calls to inform her that Basha is gone, taking along some valuables from the apartment.

"File a police report," Anna tells her.

Now a woman from Detroit has come forward claiming she had a one-night stand with JB. She even produced a photo showing them together. In the photo, JB appears to be laying in bed asleep and she is laying next to him with a smug expression. The photos of JB with Lilly are still making rounds in the tabloids. The last thing JB needs is more bad publicity hanging over his head. There's talk Benny may file charges. And amid the craziness, Anna has suspicions that Basha is behind the photos of Lilly and JB—after all, she was behind the last attempt to destroy JB. Now the woman from Detroit has thrown her for a loop.

Anna looks over the itinerary of her who's who list of clients. She notes JB is a scheduled guest on The Arsenio Hall Show. They booked him months ago, but the timing of the incident with Lilly and Benny plus news from the woman in Detroit has her making notes about what he will and will not discuss. For the last hour and a half, she hasn't been able to contact him.

Meetings with movie studio executives, lunch with a client and an hour out from their scheduled meetup at Paramount studios, she still hasn't heard from JB. She drives to Paramount and meets with the staff.

"He's on his way," she informs them and sits in the green room to make phone calls and page him again.

Something's not right. By now, he should've returned my call. The show tapes in forty-five minutes. Hopefully, he'll arrive during the monologue.

Twenty One

The following morning, JB checks the numbers in his pager and notices Anna's code several times, then he realizes why she might be calling and dials her

"Where are you? I've been paging you all morning." She's furious.

"I'll tell you about it."

"You know you were supposed to go on The Arsenio Hall Show, right?"

"Oh shit." He slaps his forehead. "Maddie flew in from Europe, and for the last day or so we've been isolated—no phone, no television. Just us."

"JB, we've been planning this for months. Do you have any idea how bad this looks?"

"I needed to see my wife, and I lost track of time, damn. It's not that big of a deal."

"Not that big of a deal? JB, this isn't just a missed appointment, it's a missed opportunity. We're talking national television, damage control, your fans waiting to see you!"

"Can't we just reschedule it?"

"It doesn't work like that. Arsenio's team cleared their schedule for you; the audience was expecting you. This is a professional commitment, not a pick-up game you can just reschedule."

"Okay, okay. I messed up. What do we do now?" he asks.

"I do damage control. I'll have to apologize, grovel, and somehow spin this so you don't come off as unreliable. Meanwhile, you need to get your act together. It's a good thing you and Maddie haven't been watching television because guess what? A woman from Detroit claims you and she had a one-night stand."

"What?" The news jolts JB upright in bed, startling Madeline lying next to him. "You're joking, right?"

"I wish I weren't. She has a photo to prove you and her were together, and JB, I saw that photo." Anna's voice is firm.

JB squeezes his eyes shut and clenches his fists. It was that night in Detroit. It was the girl who left the after-hours spot with him and Caleb. They were all drunk; he doesn't remember how they got to Caleb's house. He remembers waking up the next morning with a terrible hangover, and she was in bed naked kissing him.

"I swear, Anna. She was with Caleb, not me."

"The photo looks like you were the one in bed with her."

JB is out of bed, naked with the phone in hand, pacing.

Madeline pulls the linen bed sheets up against her bare chest, watching JB's every move, bracing for whatever he's about to tell her.

"She's lying. She slept with Caleb."

"I'll uncover the truth and protect what matters most. Trust me."

Anna's confidence is one of her superpowers. It is why she is one of the most sought-after publicists in the industry.

"Right now, I should be sporting a Chicago jersey, but this shit with Benny and now this other shit is holding up things," JB tells her.

"You want to go to Chicago?"

"Hell yeah."

"Why Chicago?"

"Why not?"

"Duh. Play for L.A. Start a legacy. Your father played here. Why not continue it?"

JB hears his pager vibrating on the nightstand next to the bed. He picks it up and sees Levy's number as well as his father-in-law, Eugene's number.

"JB, consider me your human tornado. I'll spin through scandals, whip up a storm and leave no trace. Just hold on tight—we're about to defy gravity."

"Do what you do best. I'll call you later," he tells her.

The tension in the room is palpable as JB's gaze shifts from the phone to Madeline's face. Madeline's eyes hold questions.

"Remember when we first got together, and I told you how my world could get crazy?" JB asks.

Madeline closes her eyes. "What happened now?"

"A woman came forward claiming we had a one-night stand."

The thud of Madeline's heart echoes in her ears. "Well?" Her eyes need answers.

"Lies, total lies. The biggest mistake I made was going out with your cousin Caleb. He hasn't changed since we were in college, and he's only gotten worse now that he's in the league. So of course he's a target for groupies and opportunists. A girl he claims to know came home with us that night. She was his girl, not mine. She boned Caleb, not me. I went upstairs to bed. Alone. That is the truth. I swear, Maddie. You've got to believe me."

Madeline sighs, her thoughts race and scatter like discordant musical notes. *First Lilly and Benny and the photos, now a strange one-night stand. What's next?*

JB sits on the side of the bed, gauging Madeline's expression. "I admit, I flirt and sometimes I tease, but never have I engaged in sex with any other woman since you and I have been married. You believe me, don't you?"

Madeline's frustration erupts, a tempest of emotions pent up, fueled by the latest headline and JB's indiscretions. Her elegant façade crumbles, replaced with raw anger. Each slap lands with a force that echoes through the room. JB is caught off-guard, shock etching lines on his face. He doesn't retaliate; instead, he absorbs her blows and the weight of her disappointment. His NBA-trained reflexes remain dormant. This battle isn't physical—it's a clash of hearts.

Madeline's eyes blaze, tears mixing with rage.

"Maddie, I—" he tries to explain, but she cuts him off, her fingers curling into fists. He reaches for her. In that moment, he needs her naked body to become a comforting rhythm.

"Hold me," he pleads, his grip firm and unyielding.

Madeline's heart wavers like a pendulum between fury and vulnerability. She wonders if forgiveness is a melody she can still play. Then she remembers JB telling her that her father is in town. They both need to pay him a visit.

* * *

Madeline and JB meet with her father, Eugene, in his hotel room. Eugene's eyes hold a mixture of pride and concern. Madeline and Eugene embrace. They've not seen each other since the opening night of the London show.

"Gilda told me you were flying in," he tells her.

Madeline nods; her eyes suddenly blurry with tears.

"Sit. Both of you," Eugene tells them.

Madeline and JB comply.

Eugene starts, "An envelope containing photos arrived at my church office."

Madeline's blood races upon hearing the news.

"JB told me his side. It's only fair that I hear yours."

The weariness of seventeen hours of flight, followed by nearly two days of roller-coaster emotions and physical activity are starting to show on her twenty-two-year-old face.

"Daddy, it's a case of it's not as bad as it looks," Madeline tells him.

"Some of those photos are circulating on television and in those smutty newspapers you see at the checkout lines at the supermarket. What do you mean?"

"Those photos are of me with Lynnwood discussing the tour."

"What about the one with you being pushed out in a wheelchair?"

Madeline and JB glance at each other. Eugene catches it.

"What is that about?" he asks, his gaze shifting between Madeline and JB.

Madeline takes a deep breath. JB, sitting nearby, takes her hand and holds it.

Eugene gives her a minute to compose herself. Madeline meets her father's gaze.

"Daddy, I made a choice."

"I hope," he says softly, "that the story behind this photo isn't what I think it is." Eugene hands over the picture of her being wheeled away from the clinic.

Madeline looks at it. "I'm not happy with the choice I made, but at the time, I felt it was the best decision."

Eugene lowers his head, knowing where Madeline is going with the conversation.

JB begins, "I didn't know about it until I saw the photo."

"Is that so?" Eugene takes the photo and places it back into the envelope. "The first offense is the termination of the pregnancy. Maddie, Maddie, Maddie, abortion is murder, and murder is a sin."

Eugene shakes his head. "Do you understand the wages of sin is death? Sin separates you from God, and as your father and a pastor, I don't want that for you."

Madeline sees the pain in her father's eyes. "Yes, we all sin, even me." He points to himself. "I want you to understand what was convenient for you, God might have been using that life inside of you to manifest into the person responsible for finding a cure for AIDS."

Madeline feels a tear roll down her cheek. "Sorry I didn't turn out to be the perfect young lady you, Mother and Gilda raised."

Eugene is quiet. "No one is perfect. Thank God for amazing grace." Eugene gathers his thoughts. "Second offense committed here is the keeping of secrets, which you both did, and now your marriage is suffering the consequences."

They listen as Eugene continues. "You're all on television and in magazines because you failed to handle the first rule of business in a marriage."

"What's that?" JB and Madeline both ask.

"Communication," Eugene answers. "Why did you feel it was okay to make a life-changing decision without consulting your husband?"

Madeline doesn't answer.

"And you, sir, you are in a photo kissing another woman's forehead and holding her hand. You are at her house when the husband shows up. It doesn't matter if they're getting a divorce; they are still married."

JB is quiet. Eugene apparently doesn't know about the latest news with the alleged one-night stand.

"Poppa E, there's more breaking news about me that you should know," JB begins. Eugene is silent.

"There's a woman claiming to have had a one-night stand with me. She has a photo of us together, alluding to the fact that it could've happened."

Eugene glances at Madeline before he sighs and looks at the ceiling as if in a moment of silent prayer. "Your PR team better work around the clock." He says, "I pray this doesn't affect your endorsements. I'd hate to see your personal life overshadow your career accomplishments all on account of your lapse in judgment."

JB leans back in his chair, the weight of Eugene's words settling over him. "You think that's really going to happen?" JB asks.

"I'm praying around the clock for the both of you. Your marriage is in a season of spiritual warfare. What do I mean? Your covenant is broken—that happens anytime you go outside your marriage for fulfillment. JB, you're on the road often, away from Maddie. From city to city, there are female fans whose sole purpose is to undermine the foundation of your marriage. The way certain unholy spirits work, you give an inch, it takes a mile, and before you know it, the marriage is in chaos."

JB listens intently.

"And Maddie, you're not immune. You travel too. You encounter all types—always remember the vow you made with JB."

Madeline nods, although she thinks back to certain moments and opportunities. She often wonders about the results if she acted upon them.

"Ephesians fifth chapter and twenty-fifth verse says husbands love your wives even as Christ so loved the church," Eugene tells JB. "Your wife is returning to Europe. If you don't have basketball-related plans, make plans to be by her side. No more distance. Cling to each other as one. I feel a prayer coming." Eugene extends a hand to Madeline and JB. "Father God, in the name of Jesus, have your way with these two. God, we thank you for the institution of marriage—another testament of your agape love for your creation. Your will is for marriage to thrive in love, in faith and in unity. Bless my son, JB, and my daughter, Madeline. Strengthen their union. Open their eyes to behaviors, attitudes, habits or outside relationships that tear away at their union. I pray for a hedge of protection for what you joined together. Let no one separate. In Jesus' name I pray. Amen."

"Amen." Madeline and JB open their eyes, and both embrace Eugene.

"I'm glad you both got the chance to spend a couple of days alone and I got the opportunity to spend time with my adorable granddaughter. She needs both of you too. Now I'll need to be dropped off at LAX. Ministry is worldwide, twenty-four seven," Eugene tells them.

After dropping him off at LAX, there is no music playing on the drive to JB's parents' home in Baldwin Hills. When they first got together, music always provided a soundtrack to the mood—Sade, Egyptian Lover, Prince. JB usually sang and bobbed along while Madeline sat in the passenger seat, entertained by his antics—a stark contrast from the current mood.

"I'll hold off flying back to Europe," Madeline hears herself telling him. Her words hang in the air.

"Hold off how—like fly back in a day or two or indefinitely?" he asks.

"Indefinitely," she answers. The words even cause her to shudder inside, "You need me. What kind of wife leaves a husband in need?"

Their car comes to a stop at a traffic light. Her statement startles him. He scrambles for the right words.

"Don't do that, Maddie. You sacrificed a lot just flying here. I don't want you to look back and regret this decision."

The light changes to green, and he shifts the Porsche into gear. "I'll soon hear back from Levy and Anna." He takes her hand and brings it to his lips for a kiss. "Touring Europe and playing classical music is your dream. I don't want my situation to stop you, okay? The truth will come out about Detroit, and hopefully, Benny won't file charges."

The moment Madeline and JB see Melody, the world narrows to the space between them. Their daughter, with her dark curly hair and wide, expectant eyes, stands at the threshold of her grandparents' home—a bridge between the past days of separation and the present embrace.

Madeline kneels, arms open, a smile breaking through the ache of days apart. "My baby girl," she whispers, and Melody rushes into her mother's arms, a giggle bubbling up from her joyous reunion.

JB, strong and steady, wraps them both in his embrace, his hand cradling the back of their daughter's head, fingers threading through Melody's soft curls.

In this embrace, there are no words needed—the tight squeeze of Melody's tiny hands speaks volumes, and her parents hold her as if they can merge the days lost into this single, perfect moment of return.

JB's pager sounds off. He looks and sees Levy's number followed by Anna's and Caleb's digits.

"Who is it?" Madeline asks. She and Melody's eyes are inquisitive.

"Levy, I'll be inside the pool house," he tells her when he opens the door.

Smitty the dog leaps and pants, wagging his tail. The tag attached to his collar tinkles from his movements. The door closes, and the room is still.

Madeline takes Melody's hand and sits on the sofa across from Judy.

"Mommy, are you crying?" Melody notices tears in Madeline's eyes.

"Mommy's tired." Madeline manages to smile. She kisses Melody's forehead.

"Are you leaving again?" she asks.

"I don't know, baby." Madeline's heart aches.

The words *for better and for worst* and First Corinthians verse thirteen are etched in her thoughts. She's waiting to see how this all plays out.

Judy sits, legs crossed her youthful body defies time. Her eyes are expressive, holding stories of sacrifice and dreams deferred.

"You don't know if you're leaving?" she asks, as if she needs clarification.

"JB needs me." Madeline nods. The tears she's tried holding back betray her.

"He does, but understand you're not just an extension of JB—you have purpose too." Judy's gaze holds Madeline's, and in that moment, Madeline understands the sacrifice and resilience that awaits her.

Twenty Two

B asha goes to the spot where the spare key to her parents' house is hidden, and to her surprise, it's still there. Her old Toyota Celica sits in the driveway collecting dust—the California registration tag expired right before she went to jail. Countless pictures of herself and her family hang on the walls. There is still a photo of her with JB taken during their first year at USC. They are smiling and holding hands. If only she could go back in time. She enters her old bedroom to retrieve the saltwater pearl necklace from inside the USC jacket JB had given her. She still has money from the sale of her photos, but she needs more money.

Since her stint in jail, family and friend relations are strained. She's glad no one is home; therefore, she doesn't need to explain why she's been estranged. She's tired of lugging her suitcase with all her belongings with her, so she leaves it in the closet and catches a city bus to the Baldwin Hills/Crenshaw Plaza, and from there she takes a walk.

Meanwhile, cameras flash when JB holds up the jersey of his new team. He shakes hands with the team management. There is no question-and-answer period, but that doesn't stop the reporters from yelling, "What's going to happen if Benny Manheim decides to press charges?"

"Did you and Lilly Manheim have an affair?"

"Did you cheat on your wife with a one-night stand?"

Madeline sits nearby. The narrative already paints her as the long-suffering wife. Her cousin Caleb sits next to her and explains what happened.

"Cuzzo, she's lying. JB didn't sleep with her. She was with me. She went to his room while he was asleep and snapped that photo. She used that to insinuate something happened when it didn't."

"Were you all drinking?"

"Yes. We were, but she was with me. I was the one layin' pipe—she's lying and giving him the fucking credit." Caleb's fair-complected skin is flushed red.

Madeline rolls her eyes. "You need to stop with your wild-party ways."

"Cuzzo, a leopard can't change his spots. I'm Pretty Boy Floyd." Caleb stands. He's six-eight with chiseled features and an athletic build like JB's. He gets serious. "Truthfully, whatever you did, he's changed for the better. Maybe in thirty years I'll settle down, then again maybe not. But he loves you. I wasn't on board with the relationship at first, but he is proof that a wolf can get domesticated."

Madeline folds her arms and sighs. Chicago is so cold."

"I'm in Detroit, just as cold—the only difference, he'll be winning." They embrace.

Madeline sees JB and Levy surrounded by reporters and camera crews. The constant clicking of camera shutters echoes throughout the room. Madeline feels a tap on her shoulder, and when she turns, she's met with Anna's perfectly poised presence. Her black Donna Karan wrapped sheath dress clings to her small frame. Her eyes lock onto Madeline's.

"How are you now?" she asks.

"All of this reminds me why I've never been a fan of amusement parks—roller coasters, bumper cars, merry-go-rounds. All of it leaves me nauseous, not to mention overwhelmed."

"Yeah, well, given its ups and downs, thrills, twists, and turns, it's still worth the price of admission. You agree?"

Madeline doesn't respond. Anna continues, "I don't have proof, but I believe JB's ex Basha is behind those photos of JB and Lilly. She's stopping at nothing to destroy your marriage. Weeks back, my sister, Mona, had a medical emergency, and Basha happened to be there to call for help. This happened in New York City. Out of gratitude, she was housed at Mona's for a week. Now she's gone, having stolen my sister's valuables. Something tells me she's headed this way, and my advice, watch your back. I've got a crazy feeling about her."

The names echoed in her mind. Mona, very much like Gregory Washington, III, was a friend from her days at a youth summer camp. Basha, the enigmatic beauty and JB's ex, destroyed her compositions, not to mention burglarizing and vandalizing her townhome.

"Thanks for the tip." Madeline's smile remains polite. Her guarded demeanor toward Anna has always been a delicate dance—a taut wire stretched between civility and suspicion.

When JB notices the two of them talking, his chest swells like a balloon caught in a gust of wind. His gaze flits between Madeline who embodies grace and vulnerability, a masterpiece of curves and resilience. And there's Anna, exuding confidence, her tailored suit a shield against the media storm. JB's chest tightens—a silent battle between love and ambition. In that charged moment, he wonders if he can balance both worlds without bursting at the seams.

* * *

Around 5:15 the following morning, just before dawn breaks, JB steps outside for his usual morning run. He does a two-minute warm up consisting of toe touches. As he comes up, a tall figure dressed in black holding a .38 revolver approaches.

"Shut up. Don't move, or I'll blow your freaking head off," the voice tells him.

JB recognizes the tone and cadence, and his eyes adjust to see Basha. His heart pounds to the point he imagines she can even hear it.

"Put your hands up where I can see them," she tells him.

Her finger is on the trigger. It's the second time in less than a month he's staring into the barrel of a handgun. The thought of Basha pulling the trigger has him sweating bullets.

"Why are you doing this?" he asks.

"Don't act like you don't remember, JB."

"Basha, if this is about our relationship, believe me, I never meant to hurt you."

"But you did—you used me, you toyed with my emotions and treated me like trash."

"I'm sorry," he pleads.

"How sorry are you?"

"I'm really sorry."

Basha pulls the trigger. It makes a clicking sound. She laughs at the sight of him shielding himself. "Get your hands up. I got one bullet in the chamber with your motherfucking name on it, JB. What does JB stand for, huh? Who names their child with just initials?"

"Basha, please. I'm begging you. I'm sorry I was a jerk and I played games. I appreciate how you took care of me. I was too stupid to realize it then. I loved you."

"Nigga, please."

"For real. I loved you."

"Stop." Basha's eyes become blurry daggers as her shoulders rise and fall.

"Please put it away. Let's pretend this didn't happen. Do you need money?"

"Don't fucking play with me."

"You need it. I got it," JB pleads, his hands still at his sides.

Basha squeezes the trigger, and again it makes a clicking sound. She laughs to the point tears fall down her cheeks. JB's eyes become more intense, and his chest heaves. Sweat droplets appear as if he's taken a shower.

"You see how it feels when you don't know what's going to happen from one minute to the next? That's how you made me feel, and part of me feels stupid for allowing you to have that much power over me." She breaks down. "You've lied to my face, you've slept with my so-called friends, you made me get on birth control, then turned around and got someone else pregnant."

JB wants to run.

"Please don't do this." His voice catches. "I get it. I feel your pain. Put down the gun. Killing me won't solve anything. Killing yourself won't do it either. I wrote a song for you."

She wipes her nose; tears continue to flow. "What are you talking about?"

"I write music. I wrote a love song about you," he says and reaches out to her.

"Keep your hands up," she directs him.

"May I sing it?" JB notices the anger in her eyes slowly eroding.

With the gun still aimed at him, she nods.

Seasons come, seasons go
Lovers today, lovers no more
Memories of you
Will get me through
No need for bitterness
Remember the tenderness

Your lips I adored
Our hearts we wore
Never knew our love
Could walk out the door.
Bad seeds I've planted
I took your love for granted
You'll find someone better
Who'll love you to the letter

JB's hands are still up as he kneels slowly, his eyes locked into her. Part of her is feeling satisfaction seeing him plead for his life. She pulls the trigger again. The gun fires. She misses. This time, JB lunges at her, tackling her in his driveway. The gun falls from her hand, the steel spinning before landing in the grass. He now has her pinned on the pavement.

"Crazy ass bitch," he yells.

She surrenders under the strain of his muscles and adrenaline.

"You want another assault charge? I'll tell them when they get here and arrest you. You won't earn another dime. I swear I hate you," she screams at the top of her lungs. JB hears Smitty barking.

The front door to his parents' house opens, and his father, James, appears in the doorway, his long arms stretched like a shield protecting Judy and Madeline who remain behind. "What the hell is going on?" he asks.

"Call the police," JB yells. "Hurry."

Both Madeline and Judy scream in unison.

"I'm okay," JB assures them. He has Basha's arms and legs pinned where she is unable to move. "You didn't learn your lesson from the last time?" he asks.

"Stop. You're hurting me," she pleads.

"No, I'm not."

"Yes, you are. Get off," she screams again.

JB hears James's footsteps approaching and stands beside them. He's in a robe and house shoes. "Your ex-girlfriend?" he asks. "That's her .38?"

"Get off me," she pleads.

Judy brushes past Madeline back inside to call the police. Madeline's heart pounds her ribcage as she stands in the doorway—the gunshot still echoing in her ears. She hears Melody screaming and crying and she immediately turns and runs to her room. Once inside Melody's room, she rushes to her bed and cradles Melody in her arms, the rhythmic swaying a lullaby against the chaos. She was scheduled to leave on a flight bound for Geneva, Switzerland two days ago. She convinced herself to stay as a show of support. Every day in JB's world proves unpredictable. The sound of the gunshot is too much. Madeline turns on the lamp light. Melody wipes away tears and sleep from her eyes.

"It's okay, baby." Madeline's voice is soft and assuring. Minutes later, Madeline opens the closet, retrieves Melody's suitcase, and fills it with Melody's clothes. She is taking Melody back to Europe with her, and if she needs someone to watch Melody, she will ask Gilda to take on the role of nanny in addition to being her manager.

When the police and the paramedics arrive, police retrieve the .38 revolver lying in the grass before they frisk Basha, pulling out from one of her pockets a string of pearls.

JB, James, and Judy along with some concerned neighbors watch them slap handcuffs on Basha and arrest her for aggravated assault with a deadly weapon. They check the registration on the gun—there is none. They place her in the backseat of a squad car. Her eyes lock into JB's and remain locked until the car is no longer in sight. Other neighbors standing nearby buzz with whispers and curiosity. JB declines the request for medical attention.

"Hey," James says softly. "You okay?"

JB's gaze flicked; his week has been a roller coaster. "I'm hanging in there," he replies.

James squeezes his son's shoulders before bringing in him for a hug. His mother, Judy, is present. When she opens her arms, he retreats to her embrace. Judy's eyes glisten with relief and worry, her fingers gripping JB's shirt. She doesn't want to let him go.

"I'm okay," he whispers. He encircles her, holding her close—the weight of what could have been settling on his shoulders. Neighbors standing in the yard express their concerns, and soon news crews arrive. At that point, JB and his parents are back inside.

When JB enters, he recognizes Madeline's suitcases and Louis Vuitton keepall bag by the door. Melody sits on the couch, dressed and playing with her doll. The clock nearby reads seven thirty-six.

"Where's your mother?" he asks.

"She's in my room," she answers.

As JB gets nearer, he peers inside. "Maddie, what's going on?"

She rushes up and hugs him, relieved that he is okay. She pulls away from him. "I'm leaving, and I'm taking Melody." Madeline's voice trembles. JB is stunned, a mix of emotions reflecting the sudden impact of the news.

"When you say you're leaving, are you leaving me, or leaving to resume your tour?" His eyes search Madeline's face.

"You can fly to Geneva with us or stay here and figure out your next move."

JB's face bores the weight of a thousand battles, the worry etched into his features.

"Can you wait?" he asks.

"For what?" she answers, flustered. "I've waited longer than I should."

He bites his lips. "I'm going with you."

Madeline's breath catches as she meets JB's unwavering gaze. His eyes hold a fierce determination, a resolve that cuts through the current state of their chaotic lives. In that moment, Madeline sees not just her husband, but the man who would fight for their love, no matter the cost.

JB's hands move with purpose, folding clothes into his suitcase. When he's finished, he says goodbye to his parents. A small cadre of press waited outside with cameras, screaming questions. And as Bo drives the three of them to LAX, an anchorperson's voice on a local news station reports: "In a tense and shocking turn of events, twenty-five-year-old Basha Tyree, an ex-girlfriend, allegedly shot at NBA superstar JB in the driveway of his parents' home. The incident occurred early this morning, leaving neighbors and fans in disbelief. According to police reports, Tyree confronted JB, words were exchanged, and in a fit of rage, she pulled out a handgun and fired. The bullet missed. Police arrived swiftly, apprehending Tyree at the scene. JB, visibly shaken but unharmed, declined medical attention. His parents expressed relief that their twenty-five-year-old son is safe. The motive behind the shooting remains unclear. Speculation abounds, with rumors linking Tyree to JB's past controversies. JB, known for his on-court prowess, has faced his share of challenges in the spotlight. This incident adds another layer of complexity to his already tumultuous life. Questions linger. What drove Tyree to take such drastic action? And what impact will this latest controversy have on JB's career and personal life?"

JB's pager buzzes incessantly.

"Who is it?" Madeline asks, her eyes boring into JB's.

He sees the number, followed by 9-1-1. "It's Anna," he answers.

When he finally gets to a telephone kiosk inside the airport, she answers, screaming on the other end. "Where are you? Are you okay? I heard that crazy bitch shot at you." Her voice is frantic.

"I'm fine."

"Where are you?"

"LAX. Maddie, Melody, and I are flying to Geneva."

"Aren't you scheduled to fly to Chicago in a couple of days to meet with the rest of the team's front office?"

"Yes, but listen, I need to escape for a minute. This shit with Benny and Lilly, the girl from Detroit and now Basha?"

"This is not the time, JB. Your image is in full bad-boy mode. Sponsors want no parts of it, and as for the Chicago team, it's not East Coast, its mid-west. Controversy will either sell tickets or have the conservative-minded mid-westerners boycotting. You're finally getting to be a part of a winning team. You need to show up."

"I'm already on a winning team." He looks at Madeline reading a book to Melody.

He hears brief silence on the other line followed by a long, exasperated, drawn-out sigh from Anna. "No need to thank me for spinning the Lilly and Benny Manheim debacle into a 'misunderstanding.' No need to thank me for covering up your *Arsenio Hall* no-show—blamed it on food poisoning. And no need to thank me for crafting the perfect denial when the attention-seeking whore in Detroit claimed a one-night stand."

"See, you're the MVP, baby. MVP. My ace! My homey! My nigga!"

"After dealing with you this week, I'm going to need a fucking escape," she screams before hanging up.

As JB strides through the airport with Madeline and Melody, the crowd reacts with whispers, sidelong glances, and double takes. Heads turn, recognizing the NBA star. Some nudge their companions, pointing discreetly. Others fumble for their disposable cameras, hoping to capture a piece of him. Someone screams out, "Boxers or briefs?"

JB's presence is magnetic, a gravitational pull that disrupts the mundane rhythm of travel. And amid it all, Madeline and Melody, his constants, move alongside him.

As they settle into their seats, JB reaches into his pocket. His fingers brush against the cool surface of the saltwater pearl necklace—the same one Basha had stolen from Madeline's townhouse during that fateful burglary. Madeline's breath catches as JB places the necklace in her palm. The pearls are lustrous and delicate. She traces the familiar contours.

"JB," she whispers, her voice trembling. "How?" A treasured piece of her mother's legacy, once lost, is now returned.

"Recovered from Basha."

"I thought I'd never see this again," she cries.

"I knew how much it meant to you.

"Thank you."

And as the plane taxis, Madeline leans close to JB. Her eyes shimmer with unshed tears, gratitude, and a quiet acceptance. She wraps her arms around him, pulling him into a hug. It's a sanctuary amid the turbulence. JB's heartbeat syncs with hers, and in that embrace, they rewrite their song. Imperfect, but enduring. Their lips meet—a kiss that tastes of forgiveness, redemption, and the promise of a future.

Melody, nestled between them giggles, her laughter like a bell chiming hope. The airplane soars, carrying their love across continents, over mountains and oceans. Love always endures.

About the Author

T. Wendy Williams, a Huntsville, Texas native, graduated from Sam Houston State University with a degree in broadcast journalism in 1996. "The Power of a Love Song" is her fifth novel and the third in her music series. Featured in Essence Magazine and the New York Review of Books, Williams is a wife and mother of three, currently residing in suburban Houston and working on her sixth novel.

Acknowledgments

First and foremost, I give all glory and honor to Almighty God for granting me the strength and inspiration to complete this novel. To my beloved husband, Jospeh, your unwavering support and love have been my anchor. To my three wonderful children, Layla, Miles, and Lance, thank you for your patience and understanding during the countless hours I spent writing. A hearfelt thank you to my mother, Bobbie Williams, for your endless encouragement and belief in me. To my sister, Tawanna Harding, your constant cheerleading has been invaluable. I am deeply grateful to my editor, Chandra Sparks Splond, for your keen eye and insightful feedback that helped shape this book. Marsha McCray, your steadfast support has been a pillar of strength for me. Special thanks to Mary Murray for facilitating the writers' workshops that have been instrumental in my growth as a writer. To Nancy Roundtree and Lynda Maxwell Smith, thank you for graciously opening your homes for book discussions and fostering a community of readers. Lastly, thank you to my readers for your loyal support. You all make this journey worthwhile.

www.ingramcontent.com/pod-product-compliance
Lightning Source LLC
Chambersburg PA
CBHW020510120726
47904CB00003B/765